I0771024

THE GARGOYLE'S GIFT

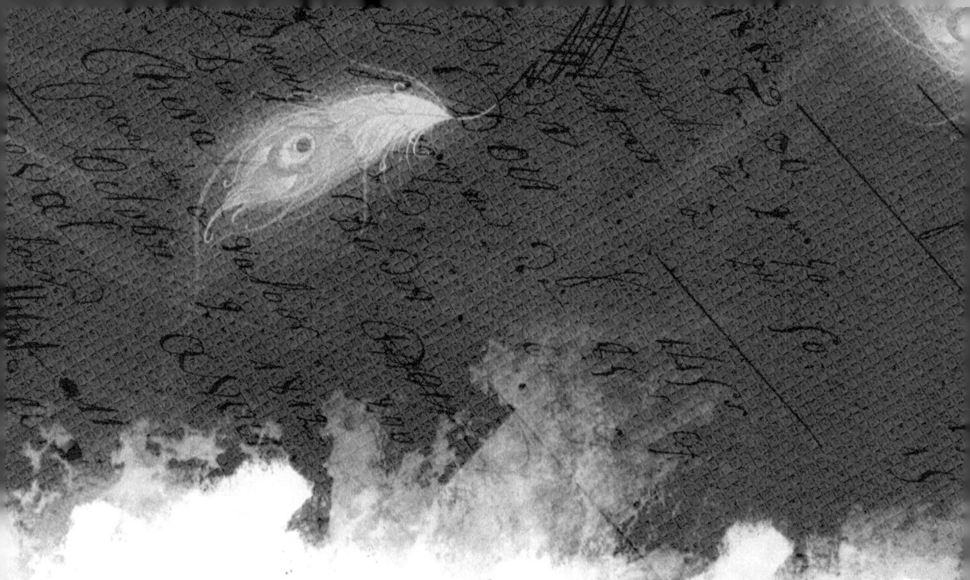

THE GARGOYLE'S GIFT

THE GARGOYLE KNIGHTS
BOOK TWO

L. ALEXANDER

The Gargoyle's Gift
The Gargoyle Knights Book Two

Copyright © 2024 by L. Alexander

No part of this book may be reproduced in any form or by any electronic or mechanical means, including information storage and retrieval systems, without written permission from the author, except for the use of brief quotations in a book review.

This book is a work of fiction. Names, characters, businesses, places, events, locales, incidents, etc. are either the product of the author's imagination or used in a fictitious manner. Any resemblance to actual events, persons, gargoyles, demons, witches or fae, living or dead, is purely coincidental.

ISBN: 978-1-958933-10-7 (Ebook)
ISBN: 978-1-958933-11-4 (Paperback)

Cover Design: Jessica, Enchanting Covers
Interior Design: Stephanie Anderson, Alt 19 Creative
Edited by: Krista Dapkey

For the sunshiny babes with a little dark side;

May you find your grumpy match

Who loves all of you, just as you are. <3

YOU

were always

MINE,

I just had to find

YOU.

—R.H. SIN

AUTHOR'S NOTE

This is not a dark romance, but there are some potentially trigger-ing themes that come up throughout the book. You can find a list of tropes and content warnings below as well as on my website.

Please reach out to me directly for specifics if needed, I'm more than happy to give details, page numbers—whatever helps you best decide if your mental wellbeing and this story are compatible.

Tropes: fated mates, secret / taboo relationship, revenge, gargoyles and demons, pseudo-medieval European setting, 'let me take care of you' vs 'don't tell me what to do', repentance for past deeds, Robin Hood acts

Content: explicit violence, gore & death, mention of physical injuries, explicit sexual content, political intrigue, mention of drugging, memory loss, brief reference to Christian-based mythos for angels / demons / gargoyles

CHAPTER 1
LOVETTE

"ABSOLUTELY NOT! JUST what exactly do you think you're doing?" I turned up the wicks on all the oil lamps on my way into the building, making the intruder flinch away from the sudden light. "You, again. Why on earth are you stumbling about in my infirmary in the middle of the night, Gaius Caledon?"

To his credit, the hulking man startled at my words, but he didn't so much as pause as he rummaged around in my supplies cabinet. "Healer," was all he offered in greeting. Several rolls of gauze and a pile of bandages littered the floor when he finally stood.

"What are you after in there?" I shooed him with my arms. "You're making a mess of things, just go sit down."

I'd been dreaming of the special lemon-and-lavender meringue pie my mother always used to make for my birthday. Of sitting in a glade, face turned up into the sunshine. Then the bell went off in my room, alerting me that someone required medical attention, ripping me from my peaceful slumber before I got to have even a single dream taste. I nearly tripped coming down the stairs because of my robe, and now I was surrounded by the stench of old ale and blood. Adrenaline and frustration had my skin flushed hot.

"I don't need your help," he slurred, staggering hard against one of the beds. The iron leg screeched as it dragged against the stone floor.

"Of course you don't. Sit." One gentle shove on his shoulder was enough for him to sit hard on the thin mattress.

Gaius was still in his full stone form, long dark hair knotted and wild around his face, greenish-gray skin cool and solid to the touch. His wings were tucked irritably behind him, but one clearly hung lower than the other, injured, *again.*

"You don't get to order me around," he grumbled, trying and failing to point a finger at me as I snatched the needle and thread he'd pilfered from his hand. Even sitting, he was nearly as tall as I was in my human skin. A logical person would have been afraid of him, especially so incensed as he was, but I was simply irritated. That seemed to be my natural state around him.

"In here I do. Besides, you're the one who rang for help, you ob-stinate creature." My hand went to my hip. In my hurry to respond to the bell, I'd neglected to put on leggings, so I was standing in just my favorite oversized tunic and lightweight robe. After giving me a lingering once-over from head to toe, he frowned intensely and let out a wobbly breath.

"Not on purpose," he grumbled. "Tripped coming through the door."

I sighed, pulling the edges of my robe together and cinching the belt tighter. "Whether you meant to or not, you woke me up. So here I am. Let me do my job."

He stretched his leg out with a grimace, the one that had been severed not all that long ago. Thanks to some healing elixir and his ability to stone sleep, it had fully reattached, but it was not the same as it had been. The blade that had removed it and one of his forearms had some kind of curse imbedded in the steel, so the limbs it cleaved through had blackened rapidly, becoming deadened and stiff. Blood was flowing again, the skin color returned to normal, but it was clear they bothered him often.

"What have you gotten yourself into this time?" My tone softened slightly as I looked at the new gash in the membrane of his wing and several deep scratches over his shoulder and chest.

"None of your business." The man was clearly tired, his haggard expression troubled and sad as he sagged into himself.

Gaius had always been a bit surly, especially with those of us related to my father. Their ages-old tension over a long-ago battle and the lives lost there lingered over the rest of us as much as it did them. The last few weeks, however, he'd been more intensely miserable than ever. Having limbs removed and getting fired from one's post by the stone kin council would do that to someone, I supposed.

I maneuvered him on the cot, having him lie on one side, so I could get the best access to his wing. "Come on then, you made it my business when you rang that bell."

"It was an—"

"Accident, sure. I heard you the first time. You're here, in any case. You know as well as I do that it'll be much nicer work if I do it, and you're rather choosy about your wings as I recall."

He mumbled something under his breath as I started making small, careful stitches through the leathery skin. He'd relaxed under my hand, despite all his complaining. His breathing was slowed and his eyes drooped closed by the time I was halfway through. Once his wing was mended, I asked him to sit up.

"Let me look at your shoulder."

"It's fine. Stone sleep will fix it."

I glared down at him, his chin sagging against his chest, body swaying gently from alcohol or exhaustion ... or both.

"Gaius." The exasperation in my tone made his eyes open. He blinked slowly, then sighed as he swung his legs off the side of the bed and leaned his elbows against his knees. I stiffened when the top of his head brushed against the underside of my breasts as he steadied himself. Stepping into him, I gently prodded at the edges of the nasty gashes in his skin as his forehead pressed into my diaphragm. That's why I was suddenly short of breath, I told myself. Plenty of patients had used my body to help prop themselves up. That's all he was doing.

"If you don't like the work I do, you could always stop getting yourself so torn up you need repairs. Seems an easy fix. Putting all your faith into stone sleep is risky with some of these nasty-looking wounds." I stepped back so I could grab some supplies, his body nearly collapsing on itself without my support. When I returned, I positioned his head to rest on my stomach, tensing as his arms wound around my thighs for better balance.

"This is going to sting," I warned, splashing some distilled alcohol over the deep, ragged claw marks.

"Burns!" He swore, breath hot through the thin fabric covering my skin, fingers grabbing at my robe.

"I did warn you." He only grunted in response as I patted the wounds with clean cloth, blotting away the mess. "Where do you keep flying off to that you come back needing to be sewn up, anyway?"

He muttered something incomprehensible moments before dropping into ragged snoring, his weight against me firm, his grasp on my clothing finally loosening.

I just shook my head and finished up. Once I was satisfied, I maneuvered him onto his back on the little bed. I gave his uninjured shoulder a good shake, his snores tapering into a healthy swear-laden grumble. "You can sleep here, foolish man, but shift, yes? So that the rest of the damage heals?"

"Don't tell me what to do," he groused, succumbing to the healing stone sleep despite sleepily arguing with me.

Once he was in his statue form, I cleaned up the mess he'd made of my supplies before turning down the lamps and going back upstairs.

I went through the calming motions of washing my hands and face, the mirror showing I had dark circles under tired blue eyes and voluminous and wild blonde curls, both from having had my sleep interrupted. I even made a cup of hot tea to help myself relax again. I found it difficult to rest when I had a patient downstairs, but there was nothing more Gaius needed from me. I pulled out my ledger out so I could properly record the infirmary visit as I got comfortable on the sofa, a cool breeze rippling the pages as it blew through my second-floor apartment.

What an infuriating man. Did he have no self-preservation instinct at all? Where was he going in order to find fights to pick anyway? He'd been removed from his council post, so there were no more missions within Revalia to report to. And because of the way his limbs had healed, he'd not yet been added back to the stone kin sentry rotation either. Yet, he'd shown up in my infirmary twice already, late at night, needing mending of one kind or another. Each time he looked far worse for wear and was almost certainly spending as much time as possible drunk.

I forced myself to close my eyes and seek the same kind of sleep I'd recommended for him, hoping to find clarity on the other side.

GAIUS WAS GONE before I got down to the infirmary the next morning. The sun was barely up, the birds mostly still asleep even, but I was greeted by silence when I popped my head in to say good morning. To my surprise, he'd even stripped the mattress and left the sheets in a neatly folded stack at the foot of the bed.

I dropped the linens in a basket to take care of later on my way to the meetinghouse for coffee and breakfast, oddly irritated I hadn't gotten to speak with him.

My sister Imogen was already at a table, her favorite tankard full of steaming coffee, a plate piled with food in front of her. She grunted at me as I slid onto the bench across from her.

"Good morning to you too." I smiled back at her. "Big plans today?"

She settled back in her chair, cup between her hands. "I have to repair a blade or two. You?"

I stacked a fried egg onto a slice of toast. "No patients today that I know of. If the infirmary were any cleaner, I'd be able to see my reflection in the floor. Do you need any help?"

She squinted at me. "You hate helping me."

"I hate being bored more."

"Mmm." Her head tilted to the side as she watched me eat.

"Who are you doing repairs for?"

Her mouth twitched as she set her cup down and reached for her fork. "Since when do you care so much about what's happening at the forge?"

"Just making conversation."

Imogen sighed and wiped the smears of egg and gravy off her plate with some toast. "Someone left their blade on the table before I got there this morning. It needs work, will probably take most of my day. Maybe all of it."

The food stuck in my throat. "Gaius?"

My sister nodded, a sly grin on her face. "Again." She clearly knew, without me saying a word, that he'd come seeking my help as well as hers the night before.

"Bad?"

She shrugged her powerful shoulders, one hand lifting her dark braid, throwing it to her back. "Bad enough."

"Same. What do you think he's up to?"

"I have no idea. And it's not really my concern, besides."

I blinked at the warning in her tone. "It could be dangerous, Imo. Whatever it is he's doing. If Gaius is out there playing vigilante—"

"Even if he is, it's not your concern, Lovette." She shook her head, frown on her mouth. There was something especially embarrassing about a big sister putting you in your place like she was ashamed of your behavior. The shame was instantly balanced by indignation, however.

"If he's going to keep waking me in the wee hours needing to be stitched up, it most certainly is." It was the same reasoning I'd given him, but no less accurate.

Imogen's disapproval twitched into a weak smile. She pushed her plate away. "You can come to the forge if you want. But you're going to be my runner."

"Fine."

My sister shook her head and laughed at me. "This is going to be fun."

The glee in her eyes was enough to make me regret my need to keep my hands busy. I could have taken a relaxing day to myself, gone into the woods and just sat with my face in the sun like I'd done in my dream. Instead, I'd volunteered for torture at the hands of my big sister to keep my mind off a man it should never have been on in the first place.

CHAPTER 2
LOVETTE

I GROANED AS I sank into the hot bath, muscles I rarely used begging for relief.

Imogen had definitely taken good advantage of having me to fetch things for her, but I'd actually spent most of my time bringing order to her supplies by rearranging the ingots and clusters of metals by size and type before cleaning and reorganizing all her shelves. While one at a time, or even by the armful, I hadn't thought I was lifting much, my lower back and legs begged to differ.

While it had been a more strenuous day than I was used to, being busy had been a good distraction. I'd also gotten a good look at the damage Gaius had done to his sword. That man was up to something, and I was more curious than ever what it might be after having seen the state of it. There were several chips in the edge of his blade and deep scratches that only her skilled hands and specialty tools could repair without removing too much of the steel.

The perfumed salts I'd put in the bath helped me relax as the soreness slowly ebbed away. I sat until the water was tepid before pulling myself out and dressing in my softest tunic and trousers. I deserved a little pampering. Regrettably, I still had to go fetch something for my supper from the meetinghouse. My apartment's food stash had been picked through a little too well over several lazy evenings, and I was ravenous.

I went down the stairs with a stilted gait, thighs protesting the whole way, one hand gripping the railing and my wings tingling their readiness to come out should I need them to balance me.

The meetinghouse was full of bodies and noise as I filled a plate and slid into an available seat near one of the massive fireplaces. Gaius was several tables over, but still directly in my eyeline. Everyone gave him a wide berth as he tossed back deep gulps of ale. He was missing a plate, however; it seemed he was drinking his dinner.

My eyes continued to stray from my plate of roasted meat and vegetables to the sharply handsome profile of the infuriating man. My fingers tensed around the handle of my fork every time his heavy cup hit the wooden tabletop.

Just as I finished up, his uneven stride thumped along the floorboards as he left the meetinghouse. I dumped my plate in the dirty bin and followed him out, surprised at how fast he was moving. I'd watched him drink no fewer than three tankards of ale with no food, and there was no telling how long he'd been there when I arrived. Annoyance crept up the back of my neck like flames as I realized he was heading straight for the forge.

Imogen had left the blade on the table where she'd found it, her lack of judgment where he was involved stunning to the point of infuriating.

"You have no idea what he's been through," she'd scolded me as she ground down the metal, giving the project all of her intense focus.

"I've patched him up well enough," I grumbled back, but I knew she was right.

I was no fighter. I'd never been in charge of making sure everyone under my command not only did their job, but optimally made it back alive, like he had. Even if that meant pieces of him were never quite the same.

That still didn't fully excuse his surly behavior, and his secrecy only made me more curious as to what he was up to. I curled myself into the side of a tree as he stomped through the yard at the forge and snatched up his blade. He gave it a quick but intense once-over, then sheathed it in the scabbard on his belt and took flight.

"Where on earth are you going?" I muttered to myself.

After a second of debate, I decided there was only one way to find out, and deployed my own wings, taking to the sky right behind him.

Gaius flew straight into Revalia, his directionality unerring despite how much he'd had to drink. He had yet to notice me behind him, which spoke to how pointed his focus was. When he landed on a narrow side street in the Barrens, I hung back. I watched from a rooftop as he confidently strode into a building with a yellow awning over the door after giving some kind of secret knock.

It was late, and the city was hushed. The noise was limited to the low rumble of adults playing a round of cards or having a quiet meal behind closed doors, most children having already been put to bed. I crept along the edge of the roof, trying to hear or see anything useful. Just about the time I'd decided I needed to get closer, there was a loud scuffle.

"Get out of here! I'll have you all reported for insubordination! Having secondary employment is heavily frowned upon, which you'd know if you bothered to read your contract."

"Sir?" One younger gargoyle I recognized from the conclave seemed genuinely perplexed as he and four others were chased out the door.

"Never return here, Varos. That's an order." Gaius leaned in, the point of his sword aimed at the youngling's throat.

They all gave brief nods, though they looked to one another for moral support, as though questioning his authority. They weren't wrong for that, he'd likely been replaced by another general, but they still respected his seniority.

"Sir, our job—"

"Is with the stone kin, not a human lender. Go on. I'll collect any wages due to you, but as of now, you're all finished with this post."

"But—" Another stepped forward, clearly confused and not wanting to lose his second income.

"I said, get out of here *now!*" Gaius shouted, blade raised menacingly. Window glass rattled, and I found myself breathless for a moment, fear skittering icily down my spine. I'd never heard anyone speak with power like that before, not even my father.

After barely another moment's deliberation, they all fled, dust flying into my face as their wings chased up gusts of wind.

Seconds later, a middle-aged man staggered through the doorway as well, wrapped in a heavy night robe.

"What's the meaning of this, Gaius?"

Heart in my throat, I leaned forward on the edge of the roof, wishing I'd chosen to perch on the one above them instead of the one across the narrow street.

"Your business is closing," Gaius said darkly.

"I've been done for the day for several hours already. Are you drunk?"

"You misunderstand. I mean your doors are closing permanently."

The man laughed. "Is that so? Last I checked my shop was approved by the councils, not to mention well supported by my community. Under whose authority are you making such an asser—" There was a wet gurgle as the man clutched at his throat.

I hadn't even seen Gaius move but promptly realized it was his blade that had silenced the man as he pulled it out of his neck.

I stopped breathing. Eyes wide, I struggled to understand what I'd just seen.

"As I've been removed from my council posts I'm here under no authority at all besides my own. You are a blight, Caster. You claim to be helping these people, but you are only bringing more despair. I will certainly be damned for my part in it over the years, but it goes no further."

The man choked on his own blood, eyes wide as he fell to his knees in the street. Gaius made no motion to help or expedite the man's death; he only watched. My instinctual urge to help the injured betrayed me in that moment, and a gasp escaped my throat. Gaius's head turned, his heated glare finding my face as my hand flew up to cover my traitorous mouth.

He bared his teeth and growled, "*You.*"

I held my hands up, glancing around before extending my wings again and gliding down to the ground. "I don't know what's going on, but you can't just leave him here like this, Gaius." I checked the man for a pulse, his blood unnaturally cool and sticky on my fingers.

"Of course not," he snipped, sheathing his sword before grabbing up the man as though he weighed nothing, taking him back inside the building. "What do you take me for?"

"Do you really want me to answer that right now?" I asked as I hurried behind him, which only earned me a grunt from deep in his throat. I didn't see anyone watching from their windows, but I knew better than to believe we'd gone totally unseen by the humans who lived on this street. "What are you doing?" I hissed as he walked through the main lobby area and into what looked like an office. He positioned the man in the chair behind the heavy desk, resting his forehead on the wood with a harsh *thunk*. "Gaius!"

"You shouldn't be here," he grumbled, throwing open the drawers. "Why are you here?" he accused.

"I ..." I swallowed, nervous and sweating from the rush of adrenaline. "I don't know." It was the truth. I had no idea why my curiosity had driven me to follow him. I'd never done anything like this before.

He shook his head, scowl on his face showing me just how disgusted he was with my presence. "Be useful then, at least, and find a bag. There should be some kind of market satchel near the door."

"Okay." I turned back to the main room, relieved to have a specific purpose, finding what he'd asked for hanging from a many-pronged coatrack. When I returned, he grabbed it from my outstretched hand without a word and began shoving ledgers and small leather pouches inside.

"More," he demanded.

"There was only one."

Finally, he looked up at me. I wasn't sure whether I preferred his stony avoidance or his fiery glare.

"You have pockets in those trousers?"

"Yes."

"Fill them." He gestured to the bottom desk drawer and moved out of my way, systematically making his way around the room, pulling things out of hidden doors and small hidey-holes. There were so many I could hardly keep track, and he seemed to know them all.

I grimaced as I carefully slid behind the chair full of dead man, frowning as I looked inside the drawer. I hadn't ever seen so much jewelry in a single place. There was no organization at all, which gave me an odd sadness. Precious heirloom rings were tangled in delicate necklace chains which were knotted on the ends of bracelets. Taking a deep breath, silently asking for forgiveness from whatever deity might watch over such things, I plunged my hands in.

"Why exactly am I stuffing my pockets with jewelry?" I asked, gut sour. I silently pondered why I'd followed Gaius in the first place, why I'd needed to eat dinner at all when I could have been comfortable in my bed, warm and safe instead of here.

"Because it doesn't belong to him."

That seemed reasonable enough. I took every piece in the drawer, jingling when I moved by the time I was finished.

He slung the bag's handle over his head and one shoulder, the fabric stretching at the seams. "Time to go." He reached out an arm to usher me forward, his fingertips brushing the small of my back. I didn't have time to process the gesture before he started knocking one oil lamp after another to the floor, setting the whole place alight.

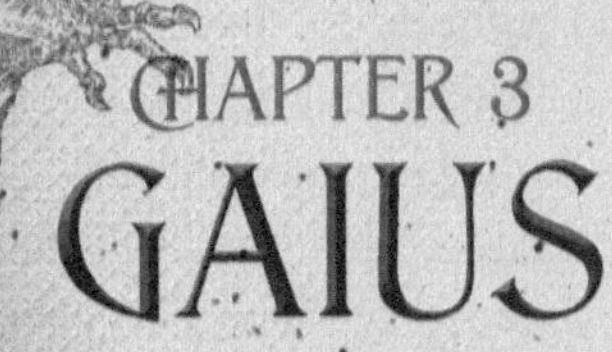

CHAPTER 3
GAIUS

"WHAT ABOUT THE neighbors?!" she shrieked, voice somehow reaching me over the sharp wind as we flew toward the edge of the city. "That building is connected to human homes, Gaius! That part of the city is too dense, they will all burn! Are you *listening*? We have to go back! People will be hurt!"

I glanced over my shoulder, finding her right on my tail, a look of concern and rage on her face as she stared me down. It was a very common expression for her, I'd come to realize, particularly when it came to me.

"It'll be fine."

"How will it be *fine*? You just killed a man, stole everything of value from his office, and set his building on fire! With his *body inside!*"

I directed us toward the conclave, confident she would follow me if only to give me the lecture I likely deserved. She yelled several more questions, but I focused on flying. I landed at the very rear of the settlement, right where the trees began to thicken. I kept a hut I preferred away from most everyone else not far from the forge.

Lovette stalked right on my heels as I folded my wings tight against my back. Everything still felt wrong when I stopped flying. My whole body went stiff, like I'd aged a century because of the injuries I'd taken in my recent fight with a fae. In the air, however, I was as young as I wanted to be. Unscarred and free to move as I pleased.

"I need you to start explaining," she demanded, hand propped on her hip as she paced the clearing, her eyes never leaving my face.

I hated that her anger made her more beautiful.

I hated that I found her beautiful at all.

"The fire won't spread. There were measures taken on that business from the inside many years ago. Stone and concrete, mostly. The fire brigade will have tackled it already."

"How can you be so certain?" She frowned.

"Because I tipped them off earlier today that they might want to keep a watchful eye on that block." I raised an eyebrow and sighed, starting toward my favored hut. "Do you take me for a reckless fool?" I regretted glancing over my shoulder as I asked the question when I found those brilliant aquamarine orbs cutting me into a thousand pieces.

She tilted her head to the side, frustration pouring off her as she stepped lively to keep pace with me. For a stone kin, she was petite, and while I was not, my damaged leg did slow me down. "Is that a rhetorical question?"

It wasn't. Not really.

Or rather, it was, but only because I was afraid of just how much of one she believed me to be. She was one of the few people who could directly challenge me and actually leave me wondering whether or not I was in the wrong.

She also made my chest ache. I didn't like it. Any of it. Or her.

Mostly.

I shook my head to clear out the noisy thoughts as my hut came into view and said nothing more until we were both inside the small structure.

"Gaius!" she barked.

I regarded her blankly, but my insides were twisting. "Empty your pockets into there," I ordered, indicating a wooden lockbox next to the bed.

She did as I asked, glaring holes through me the whole time. "Start. Talking!" She spoke in a voice barely above a whisper despite the fact that we were alone.

"The humans will be fine. Nobody will come after us. The fire will only spread through that place enough to make it look like Caster met the end he very much deserved. Never doubt, that, Lovette. He earned his fate." I slammed the ledgers I'd pulled out of the bag down onto the small table. Never breaking eye contact, she put her hands into the pockets of her pants over and over, pouring the assorted jewelry into the box.

"What will you do with all this?"

My heart clenched as a burst of rage flowed through me. Did she really think I was the monster I'd pretended to be for so long? My anger flagged as quickly as it surged. She wouldn't be alone, if she did, and I couldn't blame her for seeing me as such, even if it had all started as a ruse. Many years had passed since I'd begun wearing that persona, and I'd been very good at playing that part. So good, the lines had blurred a concerning amount.

I'd become that man, stayed him, for far too long.

"Returning it to whomever it rightfully belongs to."

She relaxed a fraction. "Is this what you've been doing? Playing hero? Trying to prove ... what, exactly?"

My chest tightened, anger rising up again as she judged me. Bile coated my throat. "You wouldn't understand."

I could feel her own rage as it washed over me. Her arms crossed, and her glare only intensified. Shaking my head, I moved my stiff limbs into a position that would allow me to sit in the small straight-backed chair.

"I am *sick* of people telling me I wouldn't understand." Her nostrils flared, and she flicked a hand out, grabbing a fistful of jewelry. "I understand well-disguised thievery just fine. What I don't understand is what you're doing, as a stone kin general, risking your neck to go into a human city in order to do … what? A good deed? Atone for your own criminal acts?"

"I'm not a general," I snapped, the edge of my words sharp. The glass dome around my lamp shook, rattling against the metal base. I forced gentleness into my tone. "Not anymore."

Lovette flinched, the barest twitch of her long lashes. Regret washed in, followed by more frustration that she was throwing me into several emotions I had no desire to be feeling, especially with no ale to hand.

"Is that what this is about?" she asked, stepping closer to me, her floral and citrus scent too soft for my self-loathing. "Some kind of twisted revenge for being removed from your post?"

"No."

When I offered no further explanation, she huffed and reached for a ledger. She flipped through the one atop the stack, stern face falling in stages as she took in the depth of Caster's corruption. My gut shifted again, recalling how many times I'd witnessed a woman begging for more time, only to sacrifice a precious piece of lace or a family gem to the money lender's greed. Men, already overworked and clearly exhausted and hungry, promising to pay double just to eke out a bit more time. And I'd just stood there. Watched. Been generally menacing as though Caster had any right to demand whatever he wanted.

I'd collected on collateral myself or assigned one of the others to do it for me. The same men I told in no uncertain terms they would never return to that job tonight. It was no wonder they were confused, I'd recruited, trained, and managed them, only to literally burn it all down. I'd been the muscle, cleaning up the mess when someone didn't hold up their end of the deal. I'd done what I'd been assigned to do, because the council had placed me at that post, and I *always* did my job. Even when it made me into a man I didn't recognize. One that was, in so many ways, just as awful as Caster.

Sometimes worse.

I growled again, the internal torture I'd put myself through for weeks finally breaching the bounds of my body. I rubbed at the place my arm had been reattached, a cold prickling pain shooting through the skin. It was never fully quiet in those areas; the unusual sword that had severed my limbs having left me with a lingering awareness of every nerve there. Sometimes it was worse than others though, and right now it was particularly irritating. I needed a drink.

Lovette stepped back. "What will happen now? What will these families do? Who will they turn to when they are so desperate to survive they have to seek the kind of help he offered?"

I chuffed. "There will no doubt be three men ready to fill the void by morning. Caster might have been the worst of them, the one with the majority of the business because he held most of the power, but there are always bad men ready to step up to be the next false savior for people in impossible circumstances." I would know, better than anyone.

She frowned again. "That's beyond depressing, but I'm sure you're not wrong." She reached out a hand. I looked up at her, surprised. "Let me see. You're worrying at it again." Her tone was so gentle, so soft, that it broke something inside me. All the anger leached away, replaced by a raw throb. It made the ache in my limbs seem imaginary by comparison.

"It's fine," I grumbled.

Lovette tutted her tongue as she grabbed my arm up and probed the healed joint with her warm fingertips. "There's nothing wrong with it—nothing obvious, anyway," she muttered, leaning her head down to inspect my arm closer. I got a face full of her golden hair, the clean floral scent filling my nose. I pinched my eyes closed, unsure how to compartmentalize how her proximity made me feel. She always smelled good enough to eat this close up, but never failed to give me indigestion. "But that cursed blade did something …" She shook her head. "Does it still ache like it did? Is that why you fuss over it so much?"

"It's fine," I groused, snatching my arm back. "I don't fuss." Truth was, the only time I could forget about it completely was when she touched me. It wasn't that it stopped tingling, that sensation was always there, but my concern about it vanished.

Everything in my head went quiet when Lovette Aurichal's skin was on mine. All the noise I constantly fought to get through the day simply disappeared. Sure, my chest felt like it was in a vice and my heart burned like a hot coal, but my head was quiet. It was addictive and wholly wrong. The last time I visited the infirmary and leaned into her body, when I was off-balance and bold enough to put my arms around her, I realized what was happening. It was a blessing I was as drunk as I had been when I figured out why I was seeking out the help of the little golden-haired healer. I was certainly not intentionally getting hurt, but I was absolutely going to her so I could have a moment of peace inside my own head.

I fueled myself for days on sour ale and the self-loathing that revelation provided. The two of us were not meant to be friends. So why did she have to be so kind? Why did she have to draw me to her like a moth to a flame, my heart squeezed hot and tight behind my ribs all the while?

"If you say so." She narrowed her eyes at me, scowling back instead of being cowed like anyone else might have been. I appreciated that she didn't bow to my harsh edges, though it would be far more useful than her stubbornness at times. "I should get back. I'm going to be exhausted tomorrow."

Sharp anxiety crept in. "Are you going to tell anyone about this?" I gestured to the ledgers.

Lovette straightened herself, chin high and proud as she took the few steps across the floor to the door. "Why, is it a secret?"

I shrugged, trying to remain nonchalant about the whole situation. "I doubt anyone will care that criminal was dispatched. Even if it wasn't officially sanctioned. Though others might have different plans than I do for such wealth."

"Then I don't see why anyone would need to know … right now."

I stiffly got to my feet and met her at the door. "I'm sure we can agree there's no reason for you to keep an eye on me in the meetinghouse anymore or follow me when I leave the conclave. I assume you've gotten your fill of adventure?"

She smirked. "Sure." Her hand patted my shoulder gently, in a placating way, like I was a child. Me, a creature at least three times her age.

Then she was gone.

I stared after her for several long moments, wondering how I'd ended up here after all my thoughtful planning for how this night should go and what exactly I was supposed to do to move forward from here.

CHAPTER 4
LOVETTE

I TOLD MYSELF IT was sheer boredom that finally drove me down the path toward the hut Gaius had claimed several days later, though annoyance was certainly a factor too. Imogen chasing me out of the forge with threats of injury for getting in her way while she was trying to work was just an unfortunate, semi-related event.

As I approached the door, my throat suddenly felt tight, and I started to sweat. I wasn't afraid of Gaius, though he did by nature have a commanding presence. That fancy voice trick he'd managed in the city had cemented his power in my mind. He was taller than me by a head and a half in his human form, and twice that when he shifted, but I was short by stone kin standards. His dark hair and piercing blue eyes leant a certain roguish look, but it was the constant scowl and dark facial hair that really sold it.

In truth, my parents—not to mention most of my siblings—were the same brand of terrifying that he was, so I was more than used to it. Besides, I was pretty sure he was actually a little afraid of *me*, if only because I was not appropriately fearful of him and had a habit of putting him in his place, especially when he stepped foot in my infirmary.

After taking a deep breath, I knocked on the door. I was expecting to get left out in the cool evening air with nothing but my suspicions and half-thought-through scenarios for where he might be. Instead, I heard a deep grumble and the thump of something other than just feet against the floorboards before the door was flung open and his scowling face came into view.

"What do you want?" he asked, eyeing me up and down.

Wasn't that the question though? What exactly *did* I want?

I'd come here with no real plan, just a desire to not be constantly wondering where he was, what he was doing, and whether or not he might be hurt somewhere. Or hurting someone else.

Instead of answering, I pulled up every bit of confidence I could muster around me and pushed past him, walking straight into the hut. Inside I was cringing because when the aunts did something like that to me, I absolutely hated it, but I was just being assertive. Probably.

"Sure," he grumbled. "Come on in."

I glanced around, finding the bed neatly made, and the jewelry half sorted on a towel lying across it. "I came to offer my help."

"Help?" He was leaning on a cane, one with a custom handle that looked suspiciously like Imogen's work.

"With ... all this." I gestured around me to the ledgers on the table and the gold and silver strewn across the bed.

"Is that so?" He crossed to the small table and took a seat, the way he moved betraying a terrible stiffness in both the leg that had been severed and his back.

I shrugged. "Sure, why not? I don't have any patients, and I'm sure untangling that mess will move faster with some additional hands. Unless you prefer to work alone?" I knew I was risking getting kicked out with that question, but I also knew odds were good he'd take it as a challenge.

"I *do* prefer to work alone," he huffed, staring me down, "but what I meant was, why would I want your help?" I waited, unwilling to give up so easily. Lucky for me, he seemed to consider an alternative option while he sipped at his giant tankard of ale. He finally spoke again, just a breath before I was going to collect my pride and leave. "You might be of some use, I suppose."

I barked a rough noise, a held breath leaving me in a rush. "Flattery will get you nowhere, Gaius."

His lips twitched, but a smile never came. "I'm managing fine with the rings and bracelets, but those knotted-up necklace chains will be the death of me. My fingers are too clumsy. They're all tangled around everything else, besides. They're slowing me down."

I turned to look, remembering how my stomach had rolled both putting them into and taking them out of my pockets so carelessly. The disregard Caster had used when he put them in his drawer was terrible, but then I'd gone and crammed them into my pockets, making everything so much worse.

"Sure. I'm good with delicate work, as you know." I raised an eyebrow and wiggled my fingers, embarrassing myself as I made the gesture. I'd turned into a ridiculous youngling around him all of a sudden and had no explanation as to why. He was an arrogant man who needed reminding he wasn't in charge of everything, and here I was, nervous to be in his hut. It was silly. He wasn't scary; he was like an ill-tempered cat most of the time. Though I would admit, the way his voice had made the windows tremble clung to me.

"I'm not sure fine stitchwork on injured flesh is anything the same as this, but sure." The words were dismissive as he put his attention on the ledgers. While his eyes scanned the pages, he turned a pretty gold ring with a triangle sapphire around the tip of his finger, the gem sparkling in the light.

I picked up a knotted ball of chains half the size of my fist. "Awful. Just look what we've done to you," I whispered in apology as

I settled onto the mattress. After kicking off my shoes, I crossed my legs under myself and made a smooth surface out of my skirt over my lap, tucking the ends around my feet. "How many have you matched up so far?"

"Several dozen."

"That's great, isn't it?"

Gaius turned his sharp gaze my way. "I suppose, though there are hundreds here. Decades worth of collecting." He stared at me so long after that, I wondered if I'd missed him saying something else. "I don't have any interest in chatting," he added finally, biting off the last word like it was offensive. "This was never meant to be a team project." He picked up the tankard of ale again, drinking deep before setting it back on the table with a heavy thud.

I flushed hot, embarrassment warring with a sudden urge to be mouthy. Truth was, I spent more time quiet than I did talking. Imogen had a limited amount of words to share on any given day, and it was hard to talk over the sound of her beating metal into the shape of a blade with a hammer anyway. My days at the forge with her were just as quiet as my days milling around the empty infirmary. If he didn't want to talk, we didn't have to talk.

Gaius exhaled loudly, shaking his head as he turned back to the books.

I settled in, pulling out several loose lengths of chain and flattening them along the fabric of my skirt. I smiled at the craftsmanship laid out before me. There were several shades of gold and silver in the mix, different link sizes and shapes. Signature styles of the artisans who made such lovely, delicate things. Pendants were wrapped up in the mess, too, some of them with sharp edges hindering any progress of untangling.

I used my fingertips and nails to coerce the tiny links to separate from their neighbors. As I worked, I made a mental list of tools that would help me with such a tedious task. Some of my finest stitching needles were at the top of the list, along with a board of nails like the one the aunts kept all their spindles of sewing thread sorted on.

The gentle scratching of a quill as Gaius marked the ledgers and the clink of the rings nesting against one another on a dowel was comforting. The hut was warm and smelled like soap and spice. Even the occasional sound of his cup striking the table was familiar.

I felt oddly at home.

"What about the money?" I asked quietly, perhaps an hour into working. It felt like a spell lifting when I spoke, breaking the silence in the little hut. I briefly regretting having done it.

"What money?" Gaius asked, looking up. He'd located and marked four rings in the time it had taken me to separate a single necklace from the knotted ball.

"The money Caster gave those people. They're getting their collateral back, right? So, what about the money?"

"Long gone, I assume. Used to buy food. Clothing. Candles."

I shook my head, realizing I was speaking incompletely, my thoughts just as tangled as the chains. "No, of course, but where was Caster getting it? Why did he have so much available to him?"

Gaius grinned. I nearly fell over when he said, "You're clever, healer. I'll give you that."

"Does that mean you know?"

"Yes."

"And?" I prompted, becoming frustrated with his truncated responses.

"And it's none of your business, Lovette. You shouldn't even know about this. You shouldn't have any idea who Caster was or that he was recently—and justly—removed from existence. The source of his wealth is the least of your concerns."

"But I *do* know," I argued, sounding petulant even to my own ears. "I saw. I *helped*, for saints' sake. So why not tell me? At least then you'd have someone to commiserate with about things. It's not like I'm going to run off and gossip about it. I haven't even told Imogen about that night." And every single day had been a new test of my ability to keep the words to myself. Every time I saw my sister and we chatted about our day, I felt like my lungs might explode from keeping such important events to myself. Chances were good Imogen knew I was keeping something from her, but she was patient.

Also, I was kind of avoiding her. Mostly I only saw her at meals and for a quick hello here and there. It was all I could handle.

"The more you know, the more danger you're in." Gaius pinned me with a stare, and it was ... soft? Almost warm. The frown on his mouth all but willed me to understand that he was doing this for my own good. It was not unlike the one my father or siblings wore in similar situations. Unfortunately for any of them, I hated being coddled.

"We're all in danger most of the time. Humans can't know about us yet rely on our help almost daily. There are demon hordes popping up randomly in and around the city. Sometimes, there are battles, fights from which many of our kin don't return. Knowing where a human criminal got his funding seems fairly innocuous, all things considered," I said with finality. I slid off the bed, setting the knot of chains back on the towel. He watched me carefully but said nothing in response. "They're likely serving supper by now, and I'm starving. I plan to pick up some tools from the infirmary besides. I'll be back in an hour or so."

To save myself any further embarrassment, and to keep him from rebutting my argument or doing something like asking me not to come back, I walked out the door as confidently as I'd entered. My heart burned as it hammered against my ribs, my pace nearly a jog as I passed the forge. I only slowed once I approached a stand of trees near the center of the conclave, my cheeks hot and my breath ragged as I pulled in deep gulps of air through my nose.

I'd spent a mostly peaceful afternoon with Gaius in his hut. I wanted to go back, and spend more time with him, even if he didn't want to hold a conversation with me. I liked the way his house smelled, the way his powerful voice moved through me when he spoke. How he was content to hold space just as he was.

And I had no idea what to do with any of that.

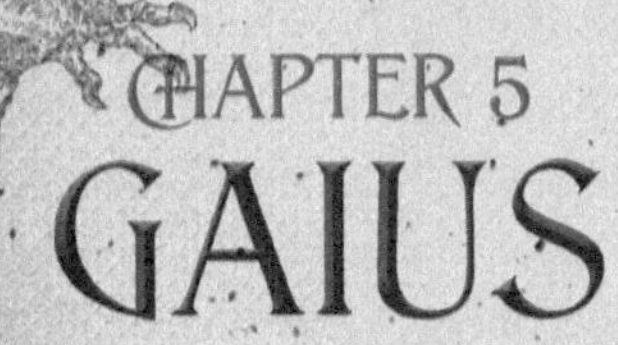

CHAPTER 5
GAIUS

THE LITTLE GOLDEN-HAIRED menace was in my hut again. She had come like clockwork every day since that first one, carting more tools with her every single time. They never left with her, either, she simply found little drawers and boxes to fit them into. She'd also only leave me alone after having accomplished whatever it was she set her mind to for the day. Sometimes it was shortly after the evening meal, other times late into the night, her eyes squinted as she extracted the final length of a chain with a self-congratulatory cheer.

Lovette was carefully fitting herself into my life, piece by piece.

It gave me reflux.

She'd also found a way to keep me fed so we could continue working through Caster's ridiculous backlog of items without me noticing what she was doing. She'd show up before midday with a basket full of sandwiches or some other kind of easy-to-grab lunch, along with plenty of fruit and cheese and enough ale to keep my cup full. The first couple of afternoons she'd left before supper, then I'd been stuck at a table across the meetinghouse from her, nothing more than a spectator as she laughed with her sister and several of the young stone kin men.

She was generous with them, freely giving her smiles, friendly touches. More than once her fingertips danced along one of their shoulders, pushing playfully, or examining some kind of mark on their skin. It should not have irritated me, but I found my arm and leg unreasonably itchy during these meals, and I drank double what I should have. I was not some insecure youth, but I also wondered why she was so free with her affection around them when she only ever sat across the room from me. It was beyond foolish and only made me want to drink more, so I couldn't think about it.

The next day, when she started mumbling about it being time to eat, instead of having her go off to the meetinghouse, I went to fetch a basket for us. To simplify things. So I could stretch my stiff leg and get some air that wasn't saturated with citrus and lavender.

Besides, she was making excellent headway through the second tangled ball of necklaces, and I didn't want to slow her progress. The sooner she was finished, the sooner she'd stop coming around.

The soft smile on her mouth when I returned to the hut with food had been a balm to part of me I hadn't known was aching. It was ridiculously primal, craving the approval of a woman for the offering of food, but my whole body came alive under her silent praise. It took my breath away, in the same moment it made me unreasonably sour, because I knew I would want nothing more than to see that specific smile and praise out of her again and again.

The next day, the pattern repeated. And the next.

It took me five whole days to truly catch on. She was clever, and I was losing my resolve when it came to keeping myself distanced from her.

"Is there something wrong with your apartment?" I asked as she separated out three necklaces and hung them from some kind of peg contraption she'd proudly brought with her before returning to the bed.

"No, why?"

"Because you seem overly content to spend your time here instead."

She paused, a confused look on her face. Her momentary blink, along with a blanked expression, had me on the verge of regretting my words.

"If I'm unwelcome, Gaius, all you have to do is say so." She made no effort to move, just went back to working on the chains with a pair of her hooked stitching needles. It was like she was knitting, but in reverse. It was fascinating to watch, and I'd spent more time doing just that than I wanted to admit. "Shall I go then? I'm quite thrilled with the progress I'm making, but if you want the joy of managing it all yourself …"

I sighed, the storm in my chest an irritation. I honestly didn't mind her presence in my space, but was far from used to the idea of having such regular company. "No. I have no burning desire to untangle those necklaces."

"You're absurd. You know that, right?" Her head tilted to the side as she quickly ran her gaze up and down the length of my body, a wry laugh rumbling out of her slender throat. "I'd be happy to keep working on these in my own apartment if you like."

"They stay here," I said, tone sharper than I intended. All of the glass in the hut gave a gentle rattle, and she glanced over her shoulder at the window.

Nobody could know about this trove. Several rumors were circulating Revalia about where all of the goods had vanished to after Caster's untimely death, despite the assurances I'd gotten that there would be no backlash or interest in finding the parties responsible. I was betting that it was mostly disappointed competition wondering how they'd missed their chance to take it for themselves, but the lower the possibility of it being linked to me, or stone kin at all, the better. Besides all that, I still had to figure out a way to get as much of it back to the proper owners as possible, and that was a monumental task.

"So with this, at least, you prefer having help?" she asked coyly, a grin on her mouth as she turned back toward me.

"Yes," I said through gritted teeth.

"Then it seems our arrangement stands." I watched as she returned to her very attentive work, carefully moving one link at a time, unbraiding and fanning out the necklaces over the blanket. She sat cross-legged on my bed again, though instead of skirts, she'd started arriving in tunics and trousers.

Her scent had become embedded in my coverlet, the bright citrusy smell driving me mad long after she left for the night, and I'd finally lain down. I wanted to extract anything to do with her from my life while simultaneously having the urge to wrap myself in her essence.

It was infuriating. *She* was maddening.

And yet the desire to tell her to leave, to stay gone, simply would not come.

SOME NIGHTS, AFTER Lovette left me alone in my hut, I continued on with the list of things I'd set for myself after the council had unceremoniously removed me from my long-held post. I had nothing left to lose except some sleep, and I wasn't all that good at resting anyhow, so it worked out just fine.

Before Caster, I'd set things to rights where a group of wealthy merchants and their army of teamsters were involved. They were responsible for throttling the flow of food and other necessary goods to the poorest sectors of the city. Much like Caster, they'd done so under the authority of the council, but that didn't make it right. I had no grace left to fall from, so the task seemed a good fit for me.

There had been more of them than I'd planned for, so it had taken several nights to manage the lot, but it was finally done. Hopefully, any enterprising businessmen with similar ideas of hoarding the most basic supplies in order to make extortionate profits got the message their untimely deaths had left. The council—who'd not only permitted such ugliness to happen but had given it their blessing—seemed unusually quiet about how one whole section of estates had turned up dead. I expected some kind of rumor about a tainted well to start circulating very soon.

Those fights had taken me to the infirmary and damaged my sword, if only due to the sheer number of opponents I'd faced. It had been nice to use my body for the things it was good at, what it was trained to do. My arm and leg were a hinderance I had yet to learn to live with peacefully, but every body that fell to my blade without me crumbling along with it was a reminder that I wasn't dead yet. No matter how much I sometimes wanted to be. No matter if I stumbled a few times in the process, literally and figuratively.

The ale helped some, but even it was losing effect, and I was growing more and more concerned that it was contributing to my increasingly weak memory.

I was no longer a general with stone kin soldiers under my command. I was no longer an agent working undercover within the criminal element on the council's behalf. I'd been the worst kind of man—one under the belief that he was doing it for the right reasons. And now I no longer had four limbs that all functioned like they should. It was all so laughable from my new perspective on the far outside edge of things.

I'd expected to be openly shunned by my kin, but nobody went out of their way to be rude or leave when I showed up. Several of the young soldiers who had been present when it happened made sure to at least nod my way when we saw one another. Mostly, I got a neutral avoidance from people. I was alone no matter when I arrived or where I sat in the crowded meetinghouse, though if I spoke, I got a response, if never a whole conversation. Honestly, that suited me fine. Nobody else seemed to even notice my damaged limbs, let alone think they were anything to look twice at. Scars were revered by our people after all, a testament to one's life experience and ability to survive. Itching and tingling sensations aside, when I looked at them, I saw the curse spreading through my veins and killing the life within, even if the flesh had returned to something close to its original color. I saw the almost-future that had me rendered completely useless, better off dead.

That was the fate I deserved for all I'd done, but the little healer had intervened, and saved me anyway.

There was something terrible festering within council walls, I was surer of that now than ever before. Someone who shouldn't be in control was pulling strings on puppets like me who had been nothing but loyal, honest soldiers. There were too many things I'd turned a blind eye to in the name of duty. Too many coincidences. Too many gaps in information that seemed vital, especially after my run-in with the red-haired fae who turned his cursed blade on me. I swore to myself I would deal with that, too, now that the supplies were flowing and Caster was gone. I'd deal with every bit of it, once and for all, whether it restored what little remained of my honor or not. I just had to bide my time a little longer.

And then there was Lovette, flitting around like a little dove, fixing us all when we needed it. Smiling while she manhandled her patients and made perfect little stitches in their flesh so there wouldn't be any lingering issues with healing ... but still a scar as record of what they survived. Lovette, invading my space, my life, my chest, my *air*.

A distraction I didn't need, couldn't avoid ... and had started looking forward to.

CHAPTER 6
LOVETTE

"I ALREADY HAVE A weapon," I argued, handing back the fancy dagger my sister had just given me. "Several, in fact."

"This one is better," she argued, arm outstretched, the blade of it in her palm.

"Imogen."

"Lovette."

"I'm going to stop coming by the forge if you keep doing things like this."

"Promise?" Her smile was full of mischief. "Take it. It's yours."

I sighed and tilted my head but put my hand out to accept the lovely yellow citrine-inlaid handle. "Why have you made me *another* dagger? One with fancy yellow stone in the grip?"

She shrugged, a pleased expression on her face. "Because someone brought me the citrine. And when I finished making it, I realized it was for you."

"But why? I spend most of my days in an infirmary. I have other, much more specific tools at my disposal should I need to cut someone open. I need some of my scalpels sharpened, by the way."

"Bring them by tomorrow then. And perhaps you need it simply because you *haven't* been in the infirmary much lately." She gave me a long side-eye over her shoulder as she cleaned up her tools.

"How would you know? Are you checking up on me?" I argued as I selected a black leather thigh sheath from her collection on the wall. "Who's doing all this leatherwork for you? These are nicer than the ones you normally have."

"Brom is the new leathersmith's apprentice. I told him I'd use his best work here if he needed the practice. Don't change the subject." She laughed low in her throat and shook her head some more as she helped me size it around my leg over the top of my pants and position the dagger in it.

Was it really that obvious? My face grew hot. Were people already gossiping about it, and I just hadn't noticed? I struggled to keep things from my sister, though regrettably she didn't seem to have the same issue. Just worrying that she knew something about my recent activities had me sweating.

I hustled after Imogen as her long legs carried her away from the forge and toward the meetinghouse. Father was supposed to be coming, perhaps Grace as well if he'd been able to convince her to leave d'Arcan for the evening.

"Imogen! Seriously, what is it you think I've been doing?"

She shrugged, unbraiding her long dark hair as she walked a sedate pace, shaking out the strands and rubbing at her scalp. "I'm sure you'll tell me when you're ready. But the aunts have been sure to mention how you and Gaius have each been taking your midday and evening meals to eat in private instead of eating in the meetinghouse." Her right eyebrow raised. "And you're both taking more than one plate at a time. Seems a little odd that you're doing the same exact thing, don't you think? Especially when the other is never anywhere around when it happens?"

"I—" It was impossible to refute that, because it was true. I had no desire to lie to my sister either. "Is that a crime?"

Imogen burst into a bright raspy laugh, her face turned upward to the sky. "You're impossible. And you know exactly why you needed a different blade."

"I'm not agreeing that I do, because the ones safely put away in my apartment are perfectly serviceable, but how did *you* know I might need a new one?" I only got a shrug in return. She was nothing if not cagey about her talent. She was the finest forge mistress around—the youngest the clan had ever seen, and the first female in more than a hundred years—but it was far more than that. She had a sense about things people might want or need, often long before they did. She told me once she could hear the metal, the stones. That they spoke to her. She compared it to music. I wasn't going to argue; I'd seen similar things with my own gift when it came to healing. I just wanted a clearer under-standing because she was my sister, and I was nosy.

As we approached the meetinghouse, I spotted our father and Grace sitting at one of the several wooden tables that stayed outdoors year-round. They'd gathered a full dinner for us already and stood when they saw us approaching.

"I've missed you, my lovely daughters." He smiled broadly as he wrapped us each in a tight hug.

"It hasn't been that long," I teased him. "And you're only a short flight away."

"True enough, but I'm spending nearly all my time in Revalia, and I miss your faces when I'm gone. Though I do have good reasons to stay there instead of here." He turned, smiling.

Grace lingered at his side, still nervous around us despite the official welcoming ceremony and vows she'd exchanged with him, it seemed. She was kin now, part of the clan, regardless of her having no stone kin blood. More than that, she was family, we just hadn't had much time to spend together yet. I could only imagine how awkward she might feel walking among all stone kin as the only human, even when we were in our human forms.

"Hello, Grace! It's lovely to see you again," I said, reaching out to embrace her.

"Hello, Lovette," she said, a broad smile on her face. "Imogen." My sister hugged her as well.

"This is a nice way to eat," I said as we all took a seat.

"Jorna seemed to take personal offense that we wanted to bring our meal out here. Something about everyone wanting to take their food away instead of eating in the meetinghouse lately?" My father looked confused and shook his head as he rearranged several things between their plates, ensuring that Grace got the nicer slices of meat and more perfectly browned potatoes. Imo and I exchanged a look, and my face grew hot when her eyebrow went up.

"Stop fussing," Grace chided as he traded her glass with his. "You never do this nonsense at the collegium." She slapped at his hand when he continued, which only made him grin.

"That's because *you* do the cooking at d'Arcan, and I can guarantee every bite is as delicious. Most stone kin aren't overly choosy about their food quality. And not one of them cooks like you do." She rolled her eyes, but I could tell the compliment lightened her heart.

"Don't let the aunts hear you talking like that," Imogen warned. "They'll get their feelings hurt, and in return, hurt you."

"That's true enough," he grumbled, but the way he glanced around confirmed he was just as worried about their wrath as the rest of us, despite him being twice their size. I'd seen them swing a heavy iron skillet once or twice though.

Small talk over our food became a healthy dose of laughter. My father was ornery, and Grace took none of his bull. They were adorable together, and while I would always miss my mother, I was thrilled to see my father had found happiness.

"We have some news," Father puffed, his hand clasped around Grace's as we stacked our empty plates in the middle of the table. "We've officially started building our home on the property next to d'Arcan," he enthused. Grace flushed bright red, the scars that ran down the side of her face standing out in stark relief when she did so.

"That's wonderful!" I congratulated them. "I didn't think that project was moving so fast. How long will it take to finish?"

"He's exaggerating a little, I think," Grace said, the flush in her face slowly disappearing. "They've barely set out the wooden stakes and string to mark off where the walls will go."

"But it's progress!" he argued jovially. "A year, perhaps. Hopefully less. Rylan has contracted several of Revalia's best craftsmen to do all of the necessaries."

"It helps, of course, that Rylan wants a new dormitory built and agreed to keep everyone on for all of d'Arcan's projects," Grace added.

"That's a lot of work," Imogen said, settling back with her tankard cradled between her hands. Tonight we were drinking a special blackberry mead Father had brought with him from the city, and I was wishing my normal-sized glass was big like hers.

"It is. Years and years. Can you imagine getting contracted to work on an ever-growing collegium campus? The rest of your life would be planned out." Grace smiled softly. "I've never had my own house before. I've always lived in an apartment of some kind." Her expression dipped for a moment, as though she realized the company in which she'd said such a thing.

Stone kin cycled through whatever huts were available mostly, we were welcome to take any open bed. Gaius and I were both odd in that sense—I had a permanent apartment above the infirmary, and he stayed in one hut.

"I'm so happy for you," I said, reaching across the table to briefly clasp her hand in mine.

"You'll come visit, of course?" she asked.

"Naturally." Imogen raised her cup in toast before taking a drink.

"You're welcome at any time, even now. I hope you know that. Calla would love to see you, as well. D'Arcan is always open."

Father shifted around in his seat. "Be mindful of Revalia. There are always things going on that I would prefer you stay away from, but it's particularly odd, right now."

"Odd how?" Imogen asked, frowning.

He shook his head, giving Grace's hand a squeeze. "People who have long been protected ending up dead. Shifts in power among the criminal element. Thankfully the demon hordes have settled down for the moment, but it's always something. It just feels ... off lately. Even the council seems unusually shaken. I'd prefer you stay here at the conclave or go directly to d'Arcan if you have business in the city."

I had no intentions of leaving again, at least not unless I was helping return some of the jewelry, but that meant little lately. There were plenty of things I was doing without really planning to, all of them involving a certain former general.

Imogen's eyes were burning holes in the side of my face, but I just smiled serenely at my father, nodding my agreement with his request. She clearly suspected—as I did—that Gaius was probably involved with everything our father had just mentioned.

"Have you seen Gaius lately?" Imogen asked, turning her eyes from me to our father.

He settled back in the seat, tilting his head as though preparing to shoulder a burden. "Not in the last little while. Why?"

"He's needed several repairs on his sword." Father's eyebrows raised at Imogen's words.

"And he's needed stitched up just as often," I added.

"We are aware of some ... grievances Gaius may be involved with. But I'll see if I can't get myself a little closer to the investigations. Is he causing trouble here?" He pulled Grace's hand into his, stroking it gently after placing a kiss in her palm. The tension around her mouth eased under his affection.

"No. He keeps to himself mostly," Imogen shrugged.

"That's good."

"Shall we take a little walk?" Father suggested. "Get the digestion moving?"

Grace visibly relaxed. "I wouldn't mind seeing more of the conclave. When I was last here, there wasn't really a chance to wander around."

Imogen ran our dishes into the meetinghouse before we slowly made our way toward the forge. Father always loved to get a look at what she'd been working on, and I was certain he was hoping that one day soon there would be a blade waiting for Grace.

By the time we'd made a circuit of the settlement, including a stop at my apartment for a quick rest and more mead, Imogen was blinking heavily, and I was not far from doing the same.

"It was so good to see you again," I told Grace when both Imo and I gave her a quick hug as they prepared to leave.

"Be safe, my daughters. And if you see anything suspect, let me know, yes?"

"Of course," Imogen promised just before stifling a yawn that had her jaw cracking.

Father gathered Grace up in his arms with a grin, releasing his wings. She gave an audible squeak as he pushed off the earth in a gust of wind, her amused laughter chasing behind as they flew away.

"She's good for him." Imogen smiled, patted me on the shoulder, and turned away, not waiting for a response.

"She is," I agreed, though she was already too far away to hear it. I was ready to find my sofa, a book, and perhaps some chocolate.

I looked up again, though, which was a mistake. It was hard to make out features from such a distance, but I knew without a doubt the dark-winged shadow headed in the direction of Revalia was Gaius.

If I followed him, I was doing exactly what my father had just asked me not to. But if I didn't go and something happened, I would never forgive myself.

With a curse on my tongue, I took to the air, thankful for the new dagger on my thigh and worried I was about to regret all my choices where Gaius Caledon was concerned.

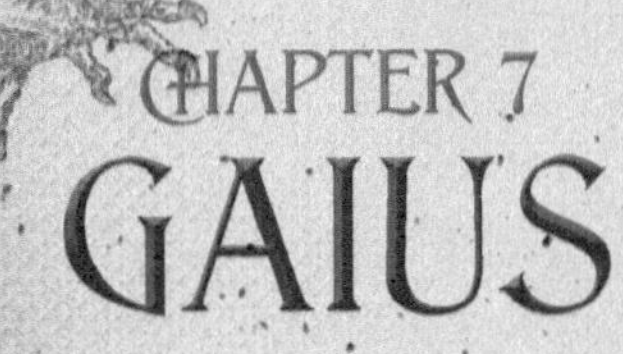

CHAPTER 7
GAIUS

FOUR GUARDS WERE on patrol at the council building when I arrived. Immediately, the hair on the back of my neck prickled. There should have been six.

I landed as silently as I could atop one of the pillars surrounding the flat roof. It was one of the two closest to the door that led into a private meeting chamber and then down into the main parts of the expansive building. Each of the pillars was ironically adorned with stone kin carvings—three were gargoyle, with their mouths formed into water spouts, and three grotesque. None of them were animate, they were decorative only, but I'd always wished I could free them from the bricks and cement anyway. Perhaps I'd get my chance soon.

Settling in, I channeled every ounce of patience I possessed as the guards performed a monotonous march across the roof. They paced down the edges of the short sides, up the longer ones, turned, then they'd switch with their counterpart. Repeat. Switch. Repeat. There was a commotion in some trees nearby, but I couldn't take my focus from the door to check what it was. Probably just a raccoon or birds getting into a row over sleeping arrangements, anyway. My chest was burning again, something that seemed to be happening more and more frequently no matter what I ate or drank. I'd be reduced to asking for some kind of remedy from Lovette soon.

Shortly after the clock chimed the hour, the doors opened, and my targets walked out into the moonlight along with the two missing guards. The fools were nothing if not predictable.

The guards dispersed to stand along the pillars, allowing the councilmen a sense of privacy near the doorway.

"Everything is fine, Hugo. The concerned members can be assuaged with some sweet words and promises that everything will be buttoned up." Augustus, a large man with perhaps four remaining white hairs swept across his bald head had always left a sour taste in my mouth.

"You seem so confident," Hugo replied.

"Should I not be? It's always worked like that before."

"The fae informant is missing, Auggie. Likely *dead*. The one who's been partnered with us all this time. Doesn't that worry you?" The slight man bounced on his heels in his excitement, making it necessary to push his wire-rimmed spectacles back up his nose with his thumb.

Augustus chuffed. "Not in the least. If he's dead, then that's one less end to tie up, isn't it?"

"Perhaps, but any who knew of his connection to us will be looking our way when they also realize he's gone missing."

"They won't, Hugo." Augustus sounded exasperated with his friend. "That fae was known for his temperamental nature and only appearing when he felt like it. Put this worry out of your mind."

"Fine, but the necklace we confiscated is counterfeit, which means the real one is still either in the possession of a founding family descendant or just loose out in the world somewhere. Do you really think nobody else will notice that detail should they go to examine it further?"

"Why would they even bother to look? It's been catalogued and stored safely in the archives. Your concerns are understandable, Hugo, but misplaced."

"Fine. But even you can't dispute the others are getting increasingly suspicious. Everything we've been working toward is beginning to crumble. Not to mention the incidents with Caster and the merchants. None of the local humans are talking, and I find it unbelievable that nobody saw a damn thing! That all had to have been Caled—"

There was another rustle in the trees behind me, enough for one of the guards to tilt his pike as he peered over the wall.

"Quiet!" Augustus hissed the word, flinging his wide arm out to silence his coconspirator.

He glanced around, posturing like he was preparing to fight, but the guard relaxed. They shifted to take positions at the four corners of the roof, one now almost directly below me. He stood rod-straight, only his eyes and head moving as he continually scanned the area, but he never looked up. Foolish and short-sighted not to consider that the enemy might fly.

I leapt over to the top of the doorway, causing the councilmen to gasp and the guards to jerkily rush in response. I'd landed too heavily on my bad leg, tilting dangerously to one side. It was ungraceful, if nothing else. I swore under my breath as they collected themselves below me.

"Did I hear my name?"

"You!"

"Me." The need for justice, for revenge, surged through my body. It felt like a thick sludge moving through my veins. I embraced the darkness that resided within me as I dove down on top of the councilmen. I nicked one with my outstretched claws as he dodged away and the others with the pointed spurs on the ends of my wings as they tried to flee back inside.

Blocking the doorway with my body, I unsheathed my sword. "Hang on now, I've quite a bone to pick with you both," I warned them.

"You'll be killed for this," Hugo spat.

"I'd love to see you try."

To his credit, he did. Unfortunately for him, he was old, slow, and hadn't shifted in who knew how long. Most members that sat around the council tables had become too used to the comforts of human life. I would go so far as to claim none of them fit in anywhere outside this stuffy, pompous, bureaucratic building.

Before he could either pull a weapon or shift into his stone skin, I had him by the throat with my sword.

"Back off!" Augustus yelled, one hand raised to the guards. The three that had approached stopped moving but held a loose formation around us. "Let him speak."

I snarled. I was not here for reason or talking. I was here to watch the traitors who had turned me into a monster bleed out beneath my feet.

Something heavy hit the flat roof. I heard a scuffle in the distance behind me, but my back was turned. Then there was a sound that chilled my blood. A very female gasp, one prompted by struggle.

I jerked my head, looking over my shoulder. My blood surged as Lovette came into view across the roof, her dagger bloody as she stood wide-eyed over the body of a guard. She swiped away some splattered droplets from her own throat, then turned to face the remaining guards.

"Stop!" I shouted, hoping that the authority I poured into my voice had some effect on the guards. It did, but only for a moment. At least their training had done that much.

"I'm fine!" she yelled back, already parrying with one of them, a dagger in her hand and her wings splayed out wide. She was not, however, in her full stone form. Her anger had been riled, but I could tell she wasn't comfortable causing harm to the humans. She kept glancing down at the body, no doubt wondering if she could still revive the man. "Please don't make me kill you," she said firmly, though her tone held an edge of pleading. The guards stepped back, stance defensive, but instead of keeping up the dance, they just watched her.

"*Shift*, Lovette," I growled, hoping she listened.

"How interesting," Augustus commented. "Isn't she one of General Aurichal's daughters? She special to you in some way, Caledon?"

Rage thrummed under my skin like a living thing, dark and fiery in its intensity. He dared speak of her like that? To threaten me was one thing, but his focus shifting to her was another beast entirely. Protecting someone else, especially Lovette, hadn't been part of my calculations. Her presence made me feel off balance, my skin too tight. Anxiety closed up my throat and made my chest heavy.

In response, I said nothing, only tightened my grip, the edge of my blade pressing into the fragile skin of Hugo's throat.

I wanted him to feel like I did; like he couldn't breathe.

With my blade through his trachea, that would certainly be a problem.

"Looks like your wounds have healed up," Hugo wheezed, the spot where my forearm had been reattached right near his face. "Quite a miracle, that. I heard there was a magicked sword involved. Rumor has it there are dreadful side effects for everything it touches. By some accounts, you should already be dead."

"Questionable how you forced the forge mistress to hand over that blade, councilman. Having it evaluated by a talented smith seems far more productive than shutting it away in the archives. Unless you were simply returning it from where it originated?"

"You sure you're feeling alright, Gaius? That's a lofty accusation. Though you do still seem a bit unsteady. Perhaps all the ale you've been drinking is having some unwanted side effects?"

I ticked my head to the side, neck cracking as the tension eased slightly. I'd thought through at least a dozen scenarios for how this would go. All of them ended with the councilmen dead. But now I worried I needed to know everything they knew before I took their miserable little lives.

"The red-haired fae. How long was he your agent?" I growled the words into the ear of Hugo, pressing my blade tighter to his throat. "He attacked me with a cursed blade, nearly took my limbs from me altogether. Lost me my job, my post. I obeyed my orders blindly for decades, protecting him. Protecting the council. So why would you still worry about him at all? What does he know that you don't want getting out? What value did he hold that you were willing to sacrifice me and all of Revalia for?"

My gut rolled, remembering the day the red-haired fae had divested me of an arm and a leg. Not only had I told my soldiers to ignore that they'd seen him do it, I'd been willing to just be done with this existence because of the injury. I shuddered. There was a blurry place in my mind when I tried to remember *why* I'd covered for the fae. I knew it had been an order, but to what end?

My anger rose, realizing how weak and foolish that sounded. When had I grown so ready to give my will, my control, to someone else?

Augustus smirked. "I told you he wouldn't remember."

Every muscle in my body stiffened. Frustrated, I realized I couldn't kill them now, not until I knew all their secrets and how I fit into them. I didn't deserve it, but I also wouldn't mind some closure to ease my own self-hatred if there was some to be had.

As I weighed my options, the sound of Lovette crying out in rage echoed off the building. I spun us a quarter turn so I could see what had happened. Her clothing was splashed with crimson, her eyes wide and arm still outstretched, though no guards remained standing. And she hadn't shifted, despite my command for her to do so.

"I asked nicely," she said, an almost indistinguishable tremor in her voice. "I said please. I didn't come here to kill anyone." Yet she had, in only her human skin. The sight of her bright-blue eyes full of frustrated tears, a streak of blood across her face, gutted me.

As I stared, I realized how foolish I'd been, yet again. Her arrival had been the perfect distraction, and they'd taken advantage of it. The doors opened and several more guards boiled out. I was shoved, weapons thrust at me from all directions. How they'd sent a signal was a mystery, but it was too little too late for me to worry about that.

My blade dragged across Hugo's throat as I beat my powerful wings enough to lift me up and away from the threat. Unfortunately, it was not enough to do substantial damage. I ducked and dodged the oncoming advances after drifting back down in a more open spot, the cowardly councilmen fleeing back inside. Several of the guards followed them, blades held out as they backed through the door.

I spun, finding Lovette ready to battle with her dagger, stubbornness and bravery pulled down around her like a shield, and a look in her eyes of sheer determination. She was not trained for this kind of battle, and there were several of them for her to face at once. And the blasted woman *still* hadn't shifted into her stone skin.

I had only a moment to decide whether I would fight them all, then chase down the councilmen or take Lovette and retreat. The slow ache under my ribs that I couldn't shake, the heartburn, the anger—I'd never uttered out loud what I suspected the cause was, but there was no doubting it now. And because of that, there really was no choice to be made at all.

It had to be her. It would *always* be her.

I rushed toward the edge of the roof, slashing and shoving as many bodies out of my way as I could. I threw myself at Lovette once I was within range, my wings flared out as wide as they would go, making myself a shield around her. If I'd gauged it right, I could grab her up against me and get us to safety before they got close enough to take a single throw with their spears. If I was wrong, I could hope that the guards had terrible aim but not much more. I'd suffered plenty of injuries by that kind of weapon before, and while not pleasant, it was something I could easily survive. Especially with her there to help me.

Lovette's eyes widened as she saw me barreling toward her, no doubt as fearsome as the angry men with spears and swords and pikes. I hit her with enough force to make us both lose our breath, but my wings held true.

"Tuck in your wings," I ordered, and she readily did so, her body soft against my chest, her arms lashed around my torso in a fierce grip, her legs twined with mine.

Once I was able to catch the wind, I flew us back through the city without pause. I didn't turn around to see the men shouting behind us, nor did I give any thought to humans who might spot us flying low through the streets. For a moment, I considered stopping at d'Arcan but just as quickly discarded the idea. I didn't want to deal with any questions right now, and both Magnus and the demons in residence there would certainly have some for me.

My chest felt like it was on fire, my heart thudding with undue urgency even now that we were out of immediate danger. It didn't feel like anger, though there was certainly plenty of that to go around.

"Months I've been preparing for tonight, and you lost me both of my targets! Why are you always places you should not be? Are you injured? Why did you refuse to shift into your stone skin? It would have protected you!"

"I'm sorry," she said, voice unusually soft. Her subdued mood worried me far more than if she'd been yelling back at me. The way she stared at me made me feel naked somehow, exposed.

When the conclave finally loomed close, I took us directly to my hut, preparing myself for whatever hellfire was about to rain down upon me while simultaneously trying to head it off with my own the moment the door was closed behind us.

CHAPTER 8

LOVETTE

I GASPED, PULSE GALLOPING in my ears as I turned to stare at him, hand clutching at the fabric of my tunic over my twisted up, aching heart.

I'd killed those guards. I was ready to take down as many of the others as I could, too, and I barely recognized myself because of it. My parents had trained me just the same as my siblings, though I'd been excused from fighting lessons at a certain point because of my aptitude for healing. But somehow, I retained plenty of muscle memory when it came to my blade.

Oddly, the fact that I'd killed three people wasn't the most concerning thing at the moment. When Gaius swept me up into his arms, my chest had flared hot, like I'd swallowed one of the bright-white embers in Imogen's forge furnace—the ones that looked pretty but held enough heat to liquify metal. My ribs squeezed tight, choking off my breath and making me feel panicky, like the powerful organ that kept me upright and mobile might not beat normally ever again. Like I might be dying.

His ranting was a muted din in my ears, competing against the throb of my heart and the white noise of blood rushing in my ears. "What were you thinking, Lovette? Every time I think you understand how dangerous things are, you prove me wrong! Following me tonight was beyond reckless, it was—"

"You're *welcome*," I snarled, my messy emotions boiling over. "Those guards were as much a threat to you as to me. I certainly didn't take their lives for *fun*."

"I could have taken care of it! I would happily have taken a few rogue stabs to complete my mission. But you ... you shouldn't have been there! I would never ask you to kill for me—"

"You didn't ask. I just did what I needed to. Besides—"

"You're not meant for killing at all, or any part of that life! You're far too good for it. My hands are already irredeemably filthy, Little Dove, it should fall to me. Especially because I'm—" He cut himself off with a low swear, running a hand roughly through his long hair.

My heartbeat thudded in my ears. "You're what, Gaius?"

The man was having a battle with himself, pacing several stilted steps back and forth as his fingers tugged on his hair. His words were muted, but heated. I caught several mumbled *not's* and *can't's*. *Don't deserve* and *impossible* both came up at least once.

"You're what, Gaius?" I repeated, throat tight in frustration.

"Fuck it all anyway." He limped forward in two long strides, palms holding either side of my face as he crashed his mouth to mine. An ownerless groan tangled in the breath between us.

His warm lips moved against mine, everything inside me going still as I fell into the moment. My eyes closed reflexively, and as he swept along my lips with his tongue, I disappeared into a glowing warm ball of sensation. Nothing felt real. My chest was molten, my ribs barely contained the beats of my heart as it surged, reaching for him. It all suddenly made a terrible kind of sense, and my insides twisted up in shock. This was *Gaius*, and he was kissing me, and I was composed of nothing more than starlight and need and—

Abruptly, he broke the kiss. Out of surprised reflex, I raised my arm and slapped his cheek with a firm *crack*. I was stunned with the revelation I'd had and angry he'd left me hanging on that horrible precipice of desire, especially after shouting at me.

I probably should have been angry he kissed me at all, but that was the least bothersome part of it all.

Gaius scrubbed a hand across his face, eyes wide. "Lovette, I—"

"You're my mate." The declaration landed between us, heavy with meaning. It stopped him in his tracks. His throat worked as he considered more words. He swallowed, but said nothing further. Azure eyes wide, he regarded me with equal parts fear and frustration.

Gaius had backed up a pace, but had a hand reached out as if defending himself against another blow. Or, perhaps, he'd simply stopped himself from grabbing onto me again. Or maybe he was halfway to throttling the life out of me for showing up and endangering not only myself but him too. I'd forced him to make a choice he shouldn't have had to make and inadvertently spared someone who might have been better off removed from existence. It was hard to say much of anything for sure in that moment.

Tears threatened again, my throat burning as I blinked several times. I wasn't sad, just overwhelmed. Something like relief pressed in with joy ballooning under it all. Fated mate matches were revered and precious. I had of course hoped that one day I would be part of one. I always assumed even those who acted indifferent to being paired with someone secretly longed to be chosen a match by the fates. But this match? Entirely improbable and unpredictable.

Gaius lowered his arm and just stood there, watching me as I sifted through the emotions crashing into me one after another. Frustration rose up, loud among the noise in my head, as I deciphered the expression he wore on his face.

"You already knew?"

He closed his eyes, blowing out a breath through his nose, hand rubbing at his arm again. "I suspected. But it was my problem to manage. You've seemed ... unaffected by it so far, and I was alright just ignoring it." He swallowed, eyes squinting as though he tasted something bad. "I shouldn't have kissed you like that."

Disappointment stung, leaving my cheeks prickling and hands trembling. Is that how he saw me? A problem to be managed? Did he regret the kiss altogether or just having done it the way he had?

I breathed in and out slowly, trying to clear my head. Since when did I care if Gaius Caledon found me attractive or skilled or any of the other things one looks for in a potential partner? I felt as though I were trapped between a dream and awake, nothing making sense yet everything suddenly clear.

"What do we do?"

He huffed. "Nothing."

"Nothing? How can we do nothing? Fated matches can't be ignored."

"Of course they can." He grimaced and rubbed the heel of his hand across his chest.

I was still spiraling through a myriad of emotions while I stared at him, his brutal beauty only enhanced by the sadness that crept through his stern expression.

"No, they can't, Gaius. Eventually, one or both of us will go mad. You know that. How long have you suspected?"

"Long enough. No matter how I tried to explain it away as something else. Anything else." He sighed and stepped back enough to lower himself to the bed. He suddenly seemed tired.

Like he'd been carrying the weight of the whole world and had finally set it down for just a moment.

"Do you find me that distasteful?" I asked, a blush heating my face the moment the words were out. I couldn't believe I'd even given them voice, allowed my insecurity to slip out.

He chuckled but there was no humor in it. "No, Little Dove. Saints help me, I swear I don't." He looked out the small window. "There are many reasons this could never work, but nearly none of them have anything to do with you, nor how I find you to be."

I hated that I wanted my ego stroked a bit more, but I still asked, "Like what?"

He barked a rough noise and raked his fingers through his hair, the long tresses falling right back over his face. "I'm as old as your father to start. Three times your age. More than."

I snorted. "I can't imagine that actually matters all that much. We both reached adulthood ages ago. Does anything significant change beyond the first century?"

"I will not justify that with a response."

"So you don't think so either then."

"*Lovette*." He sighed deeply, like *I* was the one being ridiculous.

"Gaius," I mocked. "This doesn't have to be a ... painful proposition. We could learn to like each other even," I smirked, trying to joke, but it didn't land as I hoped. Truth was, the irritating man had actually grown on me quite a lot the past several weeks. "The only alternative is for one of us to go as far away from the other as possible. And even then, eventually, we'd be headed for madness. Unless"—I swallowed—"we have the bond broken somehow? If that's even possible. We know several mages and sorcerers we could ask, but I'm guessing the only real solution is death." My natural inclination to cover my emotions with sarcasm sprang up strong but only made me feel worse. I bit my tongue.

He dropped his face into his palms and scrubbed for a moment.

"Is this some kind of test? Are you about to ask if I'd die for you, Little Dove?" His eyes met mine when he finally looked back up.

I couldn't breathe. He'd called me that before, but I hadn't really paid attention. The pet name feathered along a place inside me I hadn't known I needed touched. Between that and the power in his gaze, the question stole both my air and my attitude. "Maybe."

His mouth twitched. I could feel his answer in my bones, the fear that chased after it like a shot of adrenaline. To fix this, he'd let me take his life if that's what I wanted. It was ludicrous.

As I gaped at him, he said, "I've asked for death on several occasions, begged for it even, but I can only imagine none of those other times will compare to how badly I'll want to be removed from this plane once your father finds out we're mates. And I can't even blame him for the reaction he's bound to have."

My skin flared hot, anger and shame warring. I hated that he might be right, even more that it shouldn't make any difference. "My father has no say in the matter. Even he wouldn't argue over something beyond our control. He would be happy for me if I was pleased with the match."

His lips curled up, the smile a sharp, angry curve. "Do you really think he'll be *pleased* that the fates have matched his lovely youngest daughter with an old, broken former general? A man with no employment, no family? A man who's only gained loyalty through fear? Who's done deplorable things over and over again in the name of duty?" He blinked, as though saying the words hurt his own feelings a little.

I knew several soldiers who had been under his command, and they did not follow him only because they were afraid. He was far more than he made himself out to be in some areas and also far less. I realized right then how little Gaius actually thought of himself, how skewed his view was when he looked in the mirror.

"*General* Magnus Aurichal will not take kindly to his brilliant healer child being matched with a man such as me. A man he's held a century-long grudge with. Someone unforgivable for reasons a person as kindhearted as you cannot begin to comprehend."

I knew my father well enough to believe Gaius was not only wrong about him, but that they could work things out between themselves. Of course, that meant they had to actually try.

"Shouldn't you be more concerned with whether or not *I'm* happy with the situation?" I argued, but my tone lacked the venom I'd expected. Doubt about how upset my father might be and how I could convince him that the match was reasonable, crept along my skin like icy fingers. Indignation settled deeper, however. I'd never cared to be told what I could and couldn't do, and here we were again, debating what I could or couldn't understand. "Your gentlemanly—and I'm using that phrase *very* loosely—disagreement has nothing to do with me. You're just two stubborn men who can't figure out how to mend the rift in your friendship. Neither of you is willing to admit you've been wrong, made mistakes. That things happen as they are meant to, even if that's painful." I pinned him with a stare. "Do you even remember why you started fighting in the first place?"

Gaius chuffed another rough laugh and shook his head. "The covenants battle … it changed all of us. I lost my brother—"

"And I lost my *mother.*" My words were fiery, but I choked on the last bit, an unexpected swell of emotions caught in my throat. I rubbed my fist against my chest, trying to quell the ache that sprang up with the memory of her. "And my father lost his wife. His *mate,* Gaius."

He sighed, deflating. "I know that, Lovette. And how wonderful for him that fate saw fit to provide him another." His tone grew sharp at the mention of Grace, who, while human, was my father's soulmate and had in so many ways brought him back to life. "It's just—"

My anger rose up again, hot and unrestrained. This argument had kept my father and Gaius from recovering what had, before that battle, been a lifelong friendship. It was what kept any of us from moving past all the tragedy and pain. A silly fight, based in ages-old prejudice that solved nothing and ended up hurting everyone involved. Everyone, of course, except the bureaucrats that had picked the fight in the first place. The spoiled men who got paid to just sit back and watch the actual soldiers fight and die from a distance.

"It's *just* nothing. Loss is loss. I can't understand why neither of you has figured out that one is not greater than the other! What happened there was nobody's fault. Or, say it was. What if you could shoulder the blame? What if he could? Then what? You can point fingers at each other, at anyone else who was there, all day long. *Everyone. Still. Lost.* And there's no changing any of it. But continuing on the way you have been just leaves you stuck there. And for what? What good does that do? Are you such a fool you can't see past your ego? Here you are, angry that my father has found two mates in this lifetime, and still, you're willing to disregard yours altogether? When she's literally standing right in front of you? To ignore the bond because of some imaginary obstacles *without even trying?*"

His mouth pressed into a tight line, and he shifted his body away from me so that he was facing the window instead of the center of the room. Whatever budding friendliness that had been there for a brief moment was gone. Everything felt cold, from the blood moving sluggishly through my veins to the room around me.

My heart hurt, like a hand was squeezing all the blood out of it, when he said, "I think it's best if you leave, Lovette."

I stared at him for a moment but did as he asked, my only response the slamming of the door behind me. It might have been childish, but my frustration was boiling over. Fingernails digging into my palms, I turned my face skyward and screamed to relieve a bit more of the pressure inside me once I got a distance from his door.

Silence pressed densely on me as my thoughts raced. I needed to not be in my body for just a little while, to clear my head. When I was younger, flying fixed everything, and right now, I needed everything fixed. I needed space, air.

The cool evening breeze whipped through my hair as I let my wings out and took to the sky, my frustrated tears drying on my cheeks before I even had time to feel them.

CHAPTER 9

LOVETTE

FLYING HADN'T CALMED me as much as I'd hoped.

As I circled above the conclave, watching the trees sway and the world peacefully exist below me, a few thoughts kept coming back around. It was silly and absolutely not what I should have been focused on, but what my mind wanted to revisit nonetheless.

First of all, I'd *never* been kissed like that before. The way Gaius's lips had felt against mine had set every nerve in my body on fire. Not that I had all that much experience with kissing, but it had never been like that. And he'd called me brilliant. Kindhearted. *Lovely.* He had a nickname for me. Which meant that even if he saw the mate bond as a problem, it wasn't necessarily because of me. Despite the dark shroud of frustration, a spark of hope burned bright in my chest, under my ribs.

Right where my freshly sparked mate bond lived.

After forcing myself to stone sleep that night so I could get some rest, then nearly melting my fingertips off by scrubbing every inch of the infirmary by hand the following day, I'd stalked off to the forge, needing Imogen's advice on things.

When I arrived, I found no trace of my sister. The fire wasn't even lit in the furnace. There was, however, a man hanging up a new selection of leather sheaths and belts.

"Brom?" He spun, surprise widening his mossy-green eyes. "Sorry, didn't mean to startle you. Have you seen my sister?"

Brom was somewhere between Imogen's age and mine, tall and broad through the shoulders. He'd been in the same training class as Lionel, my twin, and had been the most talented of their year in field-dressing wounds. He had dark brown hair nearly to his waist, some sections near his face adorned with leather strips braided through. Brom was a bit of a loner, but we'd had a lovely time chatting over dinner with some of his friends not very long ago. He'd had me check a scar on his shoulder that I could have helped heal a bit nicer if he'd come to the infirmary for some stitches.

A subtle smile crossed his face. "Not in a while. I was just delivering these."

I stared at him, wondering if my sister had also been keeping secrets or if he was harboring a little crush on her that I'd never noticed. "I see. Well, it's not like her to be away. Maybe she's off on an errand. If she comes back before you go, can you tell her I'm looking for her? Your work is very good, by the way." I patted the sheath that hung along my thigh, the one he'd made that held my new citrine-handled dagger.

The one I'd killed those guards with.

Brom's chest puffed at my compliment, but the prideful gesture was balanced by the blush in his cheeks. "Thank you."

I raised my hand and turned to go, gut soured at the thought of the rooftop fight. "See you around."

He waved, and I walked as quickly as I could away from there, following an impulse to take to the air once again, only this time I headed beyond the bounds of Revalia.

KNOCKING ON THE door of Ophelia's hut brought a levity that mixed strangely with the sinking, panicky feeling the heavy magical wards around her forest gave. I'd dearly loved the time spent learning my craft under the sorceress, short though it had been.

Ophelia had what could only be described as an intense aversion to being around other people. There was no telling what mood I'd catch her in showing up unexpectedly. She was ancient, and that could bring an unpredictable, volatile nature. To be sure, existing for too long could make the most together creature quite mad. Thankfully, I'd never once seen her show a hint of the terrifying nature my father worried about.

I simply adored her.

The door swung open just as I was raising my hand to knock again, but instead of the squatty old woman I was expecting, I came face-to-face with my sister. "What are you doing here?" I blurted.

"I could ask you the same," Imogen answered, frowning.

"You're letting the bugs in, girls. Close the door, and come join me," Ophelia called from somewhere within the cozy dwelling.

We walked together into the little hut's living area, Ophelia smiling from her favorite chair as she gestured to a tray stacked with fresh bread, a little pot of butter, and steaming teacups.

"You're just in time, Lovette. This loaf just came out of the oven. I've done the honors already." I knew her well enough to know that meant there was at least as much whiskey as tea in the delicate china cups. "Sit down, the pair of you." We stared at each other from our seats across from one another. I was to Ophelia's right, and Imogen to her left. I noticed a faint scent in the fabric as I settled in, something sweet that reminded me of our cousin Greta. I wondered if maybe she and her husband had been recent visitors.

Ophelia sighed as she buttered a slice of bread. "Go on then. Drink some tea and tell me how it is you've both come to see me on the same day about mate bonds."

Imogen choked on her tea, and my cup rattled on the saucer as I picked it up. My sister blotted her face on her sleeve as Ophelia chuckled.

Mother always said that fortune favors the bold, so I sipped mightily on the contents of my cup, the faint sting from the way it burned my throat preferable to going into this conversation without the help of the strong liquor.

"May I see that weapon, child?" Ophelia asked, putting her hand out.

"Oh. Of course." I unlatched the sheath and pulled out the dagger, placing the handle in her palm. "Brom was at the forge earlier, by the way," I added, raising my eyebrow at my sister. "He was restocking."

"Mmm." Imogen's noise was bland, but I didn't miss the way she bit the inside of her cheek to keep from giving me a reaction.

"This is well suited to you, Lovette." Ophelia nodded, handing me my blade back. "And it's excellent work, Imogen. You are doing very well honing your gift. The citrine was a perfect choice." The pride on the ancient gargoyle's face was something to behold, her smile wide if gap-toothed, her cheeks crinkled. "Though I'm very curious how a healer has managed to use it in such a way." She brushed the tip of her finger against the flat of the blade, and I fought to keep from shrinking against my seat under the full weight of her stare.

"What way?" Imogen asked, tone threaded with concern.

I'd somehow forgotten how intuitive the old sorceress was. The way she knew things was often as impressive as it was disconcerting. "It's a long story."

"The best ones are." Ophelia nodded, emptying her cup. She glanced between us. "Go on then."

"I ..." I swallowed and skipped ahead, asking, "Is there a way to break a mate bond? Or could it be ignored? How long until one or both bonded went mad if they did?"

Imogen swore. "For the record, I knew you were keeping something from me."

"You've got secrets too!" I accused, defensive through my guilt.

Ophelia just laughed. "That's quite a question, girl. No, fated bonds cannot be broken without death to one of the pair. They can be ignored, sure, if you don't mind feeling like you're carrying around a hot coal in your chest with no hope of soothing the ache. For how long? Nobody knows for sure. Most pairs who try this last only decades, but some have endured without fulfilling the bond for centuries."

"There have been mates that ignored their bond for *hundreds* of years?" Imogen asked, horrified. I wasn't sure whether this information left me feeling hopeful or saddened.

"Not many," Ophelia said gently. "And it isn't pleasant. Nobody gets away unscathed, no matter how hard they pretend." She frowned, eyebrows drawn together as though she were visualizing someone specific. "Tell me, Lovette. Who is it you're looking to break a bond with? Must be someone dreadful if you're ready to go that far."

Imogen leaned back in her chair, arms crossed. "It's Gaius, isn't it."

My mouth opened, but no sound came out. I put my shoulders back, sitting up straight before nodding.

"Is it now?" Ophelia asked, laughing so hard she slapped her knee with one hand. "What a match. Though you do balance one another nicely." She stopped laughing and tilted her head. "Alright then. I see the concern."

"I'm not surprised at all, you've had some kind of chemistry with him for a very long time." My sister looked almost smug.

"Chemistry?" I demanded, oddly offended. "What chemistry? He's mostly just infuriating. It doesn't matter, anyhow, he's not interested in fulfilling the bond with me. That's why I'm here."

"Mmm. But you haven't told me the story yet, child." Ophelia leaned forward, pouring another round of whiskey tea as she waited.

Short of leaving, there was no avoiding her request, and there was no good place to start. After several moments with her staring at me, my heart thumping painfully behind my ribs, I found myself blurting out everything that had happened. My mouth kept spewing words as I relayed how I'd followed Gaius to the council building, how things had gone wrong, how I'd ended up killing three guards. I managed to hold back telling them any damning specifics about our visit to Caster's business or the resulting days spent quietly working beside Gaius, but I did include the broad strokes in my retelling. I glossed over the fight we'd had after the events with the councilmen and their guards, but they both grunted as if understanding why the rehashing of the covenants battle was a point of contention.

They both stared at me as I recovered by stuffing a piece of buttered bread in my mouth. Imogen swore under her breath again, long and slow, while Ophelia's head tilted to the side, her mouth half-smiling as though she were impressed. Admittedly, I felt quite a bit better after having spilled my guts. I'd been driving myself crazy avoiding my sister these past few weeks, and I hadn't realized how heavily everything was weighing on me.

"My, my. That's a tricky situation you find yourself in." Ophelia sat back, regarding me carefully. "Don't give up on him so easily. It's what he expects, you know. He thinks the worst of himself. Always has, but since the covenants … the decline has been obvious to those paying attention."

The ugliest of his words rolled through my mind. Unforgivable. Filthy. Deplorable.

"Not without cause, though, surely?" Imogen asked. "You don't get to be in a position like his easily."

"In fairness, he's done terrible things. Haven't we all? But nothing is that simple, even the most black-and-white situation contains many shades of gray. You know this." I did. Ophelia squinted at me. "There's more?"

I shifted in the cushion. "He also seemed very concerned about our ages. That Father would not approve."

Imogen grunted. "Could go either way. Father will more likely react how he expects you want him to. Are you going to send our brothers messages announcing the happy news? I can only imagine how Lionel will feel about it. He's never liked any of your suitors."

The only man who'd ever shown any interest in me was one of my twin's friends. My brother didn't like that I was taking time and attention from his sparring partner, mostly, and it had only lasted a few months, besides. Imogen chortled, enjoying seeing me riled up.

"They're only interested in my business when it suits them. They can just be mad for all I care."

Ophelia laughed. "Well, Magnus is welcome to challenge the match, but it will be for no good reason if he does. Though I don't believe he will—he's been luckier than most of us, after all. You're welcome to send him to me if he needs convincing." There was a wicked glint in her eye. "He always brings me candy, and while I've got plenty in my cabinet just now, I'd happily take a bit more. And I do love to see them nervous like they get when they come here."

"Candy?" Imogen asked.

"They? Nervous?"

Ophelia waved her hand. "The boys all think the way to keep me from becoming dangerous is to bribe me with salted licorice when they visit."

"Should we be bringing you gifts?" Imogen asked, frowning in her concern that we'd breached some rule of etiquette we weren't aware of.

"No, my girl, unless you feel you have something you'd like me to have. In which case, I'd take it and happily. You girls are always welcome. Those lovely women the demons have mated to as well, I'd like to see them as often as possible. They're the most fascinating creatures I've had the honor of meeting in years. But your father? Any of the other soldiers? The demons themselves? I like that they think they need to make special arrangements or risk my wrath." She faked a hiss, her hands up in pretend claws. After a beat, she started laughing, loud and enthusiastically. Abruptly, she stopped, her eyes narrowed, and she stared at me for so long I started to worry she'd dozed off with her eyes open. "Has Gaius done something to hurt you, Lovette?"

Imogen snorted. "They have no normal conversations, Ophelia. Everything is bickering. Their stubbornness is well matched."

One side of her mouth lifted. "Yes, but I'm asking about actual hurt. That kind of banter is mostly play, is it not? I would very much like to see you put that man in his place. His ego has been far too large since he earned that special place with the council."

I bit my lip, his words racing through my ears in harsh whispers. "I don't think it was intentional. He is as Imo says. Just set in his ways."

"So are you," my sister added helpfully.

"Hush," I chided gently.

"Mmm. Perhaps some space is needed. Weigh your options carefully. Leave him stewing in silence a little while. Time does many things." Ophelia turned to my sister. "Now then, Imogen, what is it you want to know about young Brom?"

My sister blanched. "I never said—"

"You didn't have to." Ophelia shook her head. "Nor do you need anyone's approval to proceed if he's your mate. Being forge mistress is an honor, but it's still a job. A job is not supposed to consume your entire life. It is not meant to be solitary work, either. You should take on an apprentice, in fact, and very soon. Surely there's a youngling with talent for you to train up. Perhaps two? If nothing else, they could man the bellows and keep the flames stoked at first, yes? And it would be quite convenient for blades and gear to be made and available in a single place, would it not? But you've already got designs on such a thing, I'm sure. Perhaps it's also time for an expansion and reorganization. The conclave hasn't been in danger in quite some time. Our kin could use with some good roots being put down. Tell me I'm wrong."

Imogen's mouth hung open. Then she did something I'd only seen her do a few times—she turned bright red and smiled. "You're not wrong, Ophelia."

Ophelia tipped her head to the side in a gesture that clearly said "I know, but I told you so" and reached for her cup.

"Oh, saints. I'm so *mad* I've been avoiding you the last few weeks! I've missed everything!" She tsked her tongue and waved a hand at me. "I'm sorry, Imo. I was so scared that if I told you anything I'd tell you everything ... and some of it is not mine to tell."

She nodded. "I understand. I knew it had to be important for you to run off as soon as we got our greetings out of the way."

"You're both very wise, you make me proud," Ophelia gushed. "So tell me, girls. What is it you seek from this old woman? Understanding? Permission? I'm afraid I'm not really in a position to provide either one, but I'll give you placating words if that helps."

Imo and I turned to one another, and we both let out snorts of amusement.

"I think we got what we came for. Thank you, Ophelia."

She smiled. "It's always my pleasure. Now go. Be happy, my girls. Whatever that means."

The old sorceress shooed us out of her hut, the wards pressing in almost painfully after the bright energy of the inside.

My sister and I rode the wind, side by side, all the way back to the conclave. Though I still had some work to do where my mate was concerned, my heart was all the lighter for it.

CHAPTER 10
GAIUS

I HADN'T SEEN LOVETTE for an entire week.

Her mile-wide stubborn streak was inherited from both sides, and she had employed it without hesitation where avoiding me was concerned.

She was never at the infirmary when I peered through the door on my way to or from the meetinghouse. There was no trace of her inside, though the whole place reeked of antiseptic like it had just been thoroughly cleaned.

I spent most of one day sitting in the meetinghouse listening to a handful of the uncles trading their tired battle stories, certain I'd catch her for at least one of the meals. But she never showed. I found myself hoping she had plenty of food stashed away somewhere, that my presence there wasn't causing her to be hungry. This, of course, just made my chest burn more. Then, one of the uncles invited me to tell my own tales, reminding me that I was much of an age as several of them, which incited a series of emotions that left me feeling enraged and like I might be sick all at once. On top of that, my leg was stiff from having sat so long, and I'd been too proud to bring my cane with me, so I stumbled out of there, cursing like the raging drunk they all thought I was.

I wasn't so daft I didn't realize I deserved her silence, but I wasn't sure how to make it up to her if she refused to be any closer than opposite sides of the conclave.

Imogen gave me a kind smile as she accepted the paltry work I showed up at the forge with. I'd scrounged up old daggers and armor, just to have an excuse to go there.

"You know, the candymaker in Revalia usually makes chocolates to sell at market on Wednesdays," she said the first day, one eyebrow raised. "I'd suggest the tin with the red ribbon."

"Chocolates? Red ribbon?" I stared at her, unsure if she thought we'd been having a conversation already, one I didn't remember a bit of.

She nodded sagely, and I left, worried my memory was far worse than I thought. The following day, she did something similar, mentioning how there was a teahouse that made spectacular muffins of all varieties, and they also sold loose tea. Chamomile and hibiscus flower with rosehips were listed specifically.

"Coffee as well," she nodded, beginning to hammer before I even turned to leave. "Any roast."

By the third day, I finally caught on. She was giving me a lesson in cheeses when the pieces finally came together in my mind. Imogen was helping me. Telling me Lovette's preferences. I left the forge shaking my head, ready to dig in my heels and proclaim I had no use for such information while simultaneously considering how best to get into the city for some shopping.

I spent so much time sitting in the small, unforgiving chair at my table sorting jewelry that every bit of me was stiff and sore. My bed was no longer a place my mind found rest, either, not with her scent still lingering in the quilt and the feel of her lips against mine burned into my memory. When I closed my eyes, I saw nothing but the hurt and rage there'd been in hers when I'd told her to leave that night. Stone sleep was a welcome respite, but even that would not always come.

Briefly, I thought about switching huts so the memories would stop following me around quite so much, but it was not an undertaking I seriously considered.

The pile of ledgers grew smaller every day and the stack of rings taller, but I found no satisfaction in completing the task alone. All of the tools she'd left in the nooks and crannies of my hut and the board with necklaces hanging from it mocked me every time I looked at them. Never mind the burning in my chest that only intensified the longer she was gone. Ale didn't drown it out, and no matter how I ran the situations over in my mind, nothing ever changed. It mattered little that I regretted saying several things. Even less that her words had struck a nerve so strongly there had to be truth in them.

I'd been a solitary operative for decades, alone with my secrets and the ego of my assumed persona. All that after I'd intentionally separated myself from any friendship that wasn't related to my work. Then this little healer came along with her inability to find me fearsome and a firm touch that removed all anxiety from my body. It had only taken her a handful of days—nothing in the grand scheme—to crack every bit of armor I wore just by being herself and constantly present in my life.

It was beyond maddening.

No matter how I tried to color it differently, there was no avoiding the truth. I *missed* her. And it was my own fault I was in such a state to begin with.

Growling, I tossed open the door of my hut and stumbled out, my leg increasingly awkward without the cane Imogen had made for me. There was something eerie about her gift, but I'd been blessed by both her blades and her tools, and I was not about to question when she'd handed it to me one day when I came to pick up my sword. I just hated admitting outside my hut that I needed help walking.

As I sat in the meetinghouse drinking, watching the young men boast and the old men boast louder, I stewed in my own misery and tried to unknot the mess of thoughts plaguing me. If nothing else, Lovette's absence left me plenty of time to sit in my own head.

I skulked in the memories of our disagreement, increasingly embarrassed at how I'd acted. Further, I was continually mortified by the primal urge to leave a basket of food, trinkets and baubles outside Lovette's door. Several versions of an apology had written themselves in my mind, but my mouth scoffed at how foolish they sounded when it tried to give shape to the words. I practiced anyway, staring into a mirror in my hut like a fool. Then I realized that it would be far easier to write it out. With a shaky hand, several discarded sheets of paper, and plenty of cursing, I did just that. I still felt foolish but my conscience was eased some by the motions.

The bond, the loss of my revenge on the councilmen, the fact that my anger might not be so righteous ... every bit of it left me uneasy.

After my fourth round of ale one night, a glimmer appeared in the muck.

If I planned it right, I could have the revenge I wanted in a very satisfying way. I could know once and for all what Augustus had meant when he said I "wouldn't remember."

So, I waited. I ate something substantial and drank the bitter brew Flora passed off as strong coffee. I left the gifts I'd finally given in and traveled to Revalia to collect outside Lovette's door.

And I made damn sure there were no golden-haired shadows following me when I flew out of the conclave and back to the council building.

IT WAS A very poorly kept secret that the archives master had an outrageous sweet tooth. I'd wheedled some extra slices of cake from Jorna on my way out of the meetinghouse, claiming it helped with my digestion. She'd rolled her eyes but still packed them up in heavy paper for me and sent me on my way. One I left in the basket full of things I'd set outside Lovette's apartment door, and the other was hopefully a passkey into the archives.

Sol shifted foot to foot, visibly uncomfortable when I appeared in front of him. "Gaius. I didn't realize your privileges had been reinstated, welcome back." He widened his stance in front of the intricately carved double doors that led to the archives, eyeing the package I carried.

"You know they can't ever make up their minds," I said, offering the cake. "Jorna sends her regards as well."

He licked his lips, hand stretching out to receive the bundle greedily. "It has been a long while since I enjoyed the hospitality of the conclave. Give her my thanks."

"Of course." I gestured to the doors behind him. "I'm expected."

Sol's head tilted to the side, his eyes narrowing suspiciously. "They never have anyone else with them."

Idiot. He'd just confirmed that they were indeed inside, having a meeting. That they did so regularly.

"They sent for me. New assignment."

While he considered, he unwrapped the cake, blatantly salivating over the cinnamon and sugar confection.

"What's the passcode?"

I covered my anxiety with anger. "Are you being serious?"

"Just doing my job, Gaius." He shrugged.

I shook my head and considered making a grab for the cake. But I knew these men, knew their egos and the way they would only use something they too could easily recall.

"Clandestine," I guessed, infusing the word with as much confidence as possible.

He smirked, shaking his head as he leaned his face into the cake. "Go on," he mumbled over the bite, stepping aside as he pushed open the double doors.

How people who were nothing if not predictable constantly got away with the conspiracy they did was beyond me. As expected, Hugo and Augustus were in the smallest room of the archives, sitting at a round marble-topped table, gossiping loudly about their latest exploits in Revalia.

I crept around corners and hugged the shadows as they dropped my name yet again, telling me everything I needed to know about how informed the council at large was about what happened on the roof.

"No need to raise alarms, the guards have all been debriefed. They were all dosed as well. What happened will remain a secret."

"You are too confident in that magic, Auggie. There were a dozen men up there, all of them saw two stone kin escape. Stone kin who threatened us and killed our men. Do you truly think a little potion is going to keep them quiet forever? That none of them will have even a shred of recollection?"

"It's worked so far, hasn't it? Lots of folks have been dosed for years, Caledon included. You worry too much."

My blood turned to ice hearing my name. They'd been drugging me? For years? That had to be what they'd meant by me not remembering. Horror warred with relief. While I wanted to latch on to the idea that I hadn't been fully responsible for the things I'd done, the person I'd become because it was who I'd pretended to be, it didn't change anything.

As I crept closer, Hugo grumbled to himself, drinking from a ridiculously dainty cup of tea. I lingered in the shadows for nearly an hour, listening to them talk entirely too freely about exploits that were beyond damning. Simply killing them would not be enough. They needed to face the larger council for their crimes. And I needed a new plan.

Every nerve bristled, because this was not something I could accomplish alone. I needed allies, help, and the backing of as many other council members as I could get. Something I'd done the opposite of cultivate all these years.

Which meant at the very least, I needed to speak with Magnus. My skin itched at the thought, but there was no way around it. He had the position, the power, and the logical mind to help me sort this out.

While they wrapped up their little gossip session, I blended further back into the shadows and made my way toward the door.

When I waked back through, Sol was nowhere to be found. Cursing his untidiness, I used my foot to scatter the pile of cake crumbs he'd left on the floor and strode through the council building with enough haste to not be bothered by any passersby but not so much it would raise concern.

As I turned the final corner before the staircase to freedom, I nearly stumbled, and not because I still refused to use my cane in public. I should have known things were going far too smoothly.

Magnus stepped out of the double doors to one of the council chambers down the long hall, our eyes meeting as I continued on my way. Fate was playing games with me, that was the only explanation. It was as though my thoughts had summoned him, but I hadn't yet even had time to settle into the idea of having to talk to him, let alone organized what I wanted to say.

"Gaius?" he asked, looking around. "What brings you here?"

"Same as you," I groused, continuing on toward the stairs.

"I doubt that very much." Magnus grunted. "Have a moment?"

My initial reaction almost had me blurting, *"Not really,"* but I gritted my jaw and ground out, "I suppose," instead.

"Good. I've several questions I need to ask you. Shall we go to the Empty Cask? We could have a drink. I'd say like old times, but there weren't many of those."

His candor got half a smile out of me. "I suppose I could join you for an ale."

He nodded, and we departed the council building together, nervous energy humming under my skin.

CHAPTER 11
GAIUS

THE WAITRESS HAD barely set the tankards in front of us before Magnus started right in.

"I assume there's a reasonable explanation as to why you're connected to several unusual occurrences within the walls of this city as of late?" His tone held no condemnation, and his eyebrow lifted with something like amusement as he brought his ale to his mouth.

"Define *reasonable*."

Magnus snorted, then shook his head and relaxed back in his chair. "You know, my niece is quite wise for being just a youngling."

"Niece?" I frowned at him. This chat was already proving far more disjointed than I was prepared to manage. I understood now where Imogen got her conversational skills.

"Yes, Greta. She's mated to the white-haired demon who helped us with the horde that managed to get inside the city gate?"

I nodded. I wasn't daft. "Yes, I know who she is, I just didn't think we were here to talk about your relations. Or their mates."

The bond flared under my ribs, my thoughts straying to Lovette at the mere mention of the word.

"I have a point, I promise. She told me I had to make things right, even if I didn't know where to start."

The back of my neck tingled, a warning of what he was on about. "Make what right?"

Magnus was as uncomfortable as I was, his hands clenching and unclenching around his ale tankard, his body shifting position in his chair. "This." He gestured between us with one hand. "My discord with you, Gaius. For the things that have driven us apart all these years. It is foolish to continue allowing what happened to come between us when we could have long since been allies. Friends." He glanced down, focused on something carved into the tabletop instead of looking me in the eye. "We have to forgive one another. It's well past time."

I scoffed, unable to censor my knee-jerk reaction to such a suggestion. But it was no different than what Lovette had told me, and in truth, since he and I had gotten into a brawl outside of Caster's shop not long ago, regret had festered away inside me.

"You broke my nose, you know," I said, hearkening back to that day. We'd had an altercation in the street, several punches thrown and landed between us. Blood spilled. And revelations on both sides.

"Looks like it healed up fine. It's no more crooked than it has always been." Magnus smirked, but it was short-lived. "There are things I cannot move past, regarding Grace. I am on her timeline where her history with you is concerned. Ours is a separate thing. I'm sure you understand."

I adjusted my aching leg, shame cool as it swirled through my veins. I'd unintentionally terrorized his mate, believing I was flirting. Setting us up to be something far more than we were ever meant to be in my mind only. I'd needed a new perspective on my actions to see what I was doing, to realize how far I'd fallen into my assumed persona while I worked for Caster under the blessing of the council.

I gulped deep from my cup, the heat settling in my chest as I formed the necessary words. Words that tasted like ashes but left me feeling lighter once they were out. "I do. And I am sorry, to the both of you, for how I behaved. You were right, I had every opportunity to make choices that would have actually been helpful to her and did not. If you could extend my apologies to her, I'd appreciate it."

"Oh," Magnus said, mouth agape. "I will, of course."

I nodded, finishing the contents of my cup and raising it to signal the waitress I needed a refill. She hurried over with a pitcher, filling my cup and his with a smile. In the back of my mind, I conjured Lovette's face, a smile on her lips. My heart thumped at the idea of making her proud. I shook my head, clearing thoughts of her away so I could focus on her father, but the burn under my ribs refused to abate.

"Which brings us to the several other things we need to discuss, Gaius. Do you happen to know anything about what happened to Caster or his shop?" I stared across the table, saying nothing as I sipped at my refreshed ale. "I see. Was what happened sanctioned? Like your employment there?"

I snorted. "Hardly."

"And the merchants?"

"What merchants?" I tilted my head to the side, playing dumb, curious to find how much he'd discovered.

"The ones who all had estates on that street with the faulty well."

His levity, not to mention the excuse I'd known would be used, made me laugh. "Seems like several items are much more readily available in town since they met their untimely end."

"Indeed." He settled back in his chair again, the tension between us having relaxed to a much more comfortable level. "Listen, Gaius. What happened at covenants—"

"Should be left in the past." I forced the words out, trying to avoid any chance of keeping them in. I could see Lovette again in my mind, smiling at me. Craving her approval so desperately was an annoyance, but it was one I found myself growing used to little by little.

"I ..." Magnus frowned, his eyes widening. "Yes. I agree. I came to say the same. That I have regretted many things that happened that day, but I should not blame you for them. Ygritte would be very cross with me for continuing to hold a grudge over what happened. She met her end as she wished, and there is no one at fault for it save the creature she was battling at the time." His features went still, his focus once again on the table instead of me.

I could easily guess what he was seeing in the wood—the faces of those we lost that day, the enemies that bested us if only for long enough to take many dear to us. I thought of my brother who'd fallen to a blade that should have been easily deflected. A blade that turned his veins black ...

The memory startled me. My ale sloshed over the rim of my cup, drawing Magnus's attention. As the bubbles popped on the tabletop, I wondered why such an important detail had evaded me until now. "Magnus, that sword, the one that was used on me, did Imogen have a chance to evaluate it before the council forced her to turn it in?"

He nodded. "Yes. It's much older, obviously, but was fabricated much like the one she made for my niece. Not quite the same, however. There were elements she hadn't been able to separate out from her sample when it was confiscated." Magnus tilted his head, scanning my face. "What are you thinking?"

"Do you recall ever seeing a blade like that before? One that does what it did to me?"

Magnus shook his head. "No. But something tells me you have?"

"Yes. Though ..." I didn't know how to explain the new memory. Wasn't sure it was even real, though it felt more honest than many things the past several decades. "Do you have faith in our council, Magnus?"

His mouth turned downward. "No."

The simple, firm admission affirmed all the reasons we'd once been allies. Friends. We were not so different, even after all the distance we'd put between ourselves.

"Good. There's rot there, and it's spreading."

Magnus nodded. "I made the mistake of giving a full report during debrief and mentioned the sword before I could censor myself. I'm the reason it's in the archives instead of where it belongs—safe at the conclave or perhaps even with the archmage."

"Mmm. They've trained us too well after all these years. I actually have good reason to believe they've been drugging some of us into forgetfulness." I frowned as the words came out, feeling foolish despite not being at fault for something well beyond my control.

"What?"

I drank deep again, preparing to admit things to Magnus I'd barely had a chance to get my own mind around. "I've overheard Hugo and Augustus talking. It's come up more than once. It would explain several things."

"Mmm." Magnus rubbed his chin thoughtfully. "What are you suggesting?"

"We need to expose and excise the disease," I said, using words I'd head Lovette say in the infirmary more than once.

"But first we need to know how deep it's invaded." Magnus nodded. "What have you remembered, Gaius?"

I stared at him for a moment, steeling myself to forge a thread of friendship and trust between us. "Brutus ... his flesh turned black before he died, much like mine did when that sword severed my limbs."

Magnus's eyebrows drew together. He tossed a glance over his shoulder, making sure we were not being observed. We'd been seated in a private corner, but one never could tell in such places. "Are you sure?"

"Yes. It's only just returned to me, but I know it to be true. I can remember being horrified at the time, wondering what terrible magic was at play. I cannot be sure when I forgot that detail, but it must have been soon after." My skin crawled, considering what else I'd conveniently lost from my recollection over the years. "What about you, were there any injured you can recall suffering the same affliction?"

He frowned harder. "No, but we were not in the same part of the battlefield." He leaned forward, voice lower still. "There was a book I obtained from the archives, a journal. It detailed the beginnings of the council. Have you read anything like that?" I shook my head. "It went through, in real-time entries, how in the beginning, the goals of the founding members were pure. Lofty but well-intentioned. Then the power began corrupting, little by little. There's a reason such a record was locked away. Perhaps we can avail ourselves of the knowledge and improve things, if we work together."

He'd read my mind. "I'd love to read such a book for myself, if you still have it? There are two members I know for sure are operating under only their own motives. What's to say it's not more? Or all?" I fought the urge to shudder under the implication of such a thing.

"Indeed. There's a history of disappearances—people and items alike—when they were seen as problematic to the council's goals. Be cautious, Gaius."

"Are you telling me I should play nice, Magnus?"

He snorted. "I suppose, though I'm assuming it's already too late?"

I didn't justify the comment with a response, just inclined my head and drank more ale. My arm had begun to ache, but I forced myself not to touch it.

"Greta may have an elixir to help restore memories," he muttered thoughtfully. "I'll speak with her."

Silence fell over our table while we both considered what we'd learned. Then the scheming began, and there were few things more dangerous than two well-battled generals who had reason to believe the ones handing down their orders were self-motivated traitors.

By the time we were finished strategizing, we'd ordered several more drinks plus the equivalent of a second supper. In thanks for her attention and our privacy, we'd tipped the waitress more coin than she likely saw in a full night's work. We'd also come to detailed decisions on when and how we should make our move on the councilmen and two contingency plans just in case anything went sideways. It was invigorating in a way only battle planning could be.

"I'm glad to have you back, old friend." Magnus slapped me hard on the shoulder as we made our way to a part of the city where we could take to the rooftops and sky without being seen.

I didn't know what to say in response, but I felt lighter than I had in ages. Proud. Like I still deserved to have a place among my people. Like I had a sense of direction.

And it was taking me right back to the conclave, toward Lovette.

Chapter 12
Lovette

I SHOULDN'T HAVE BEEN so pleased to find Gaius's gift sitting outside my apartment door after my late dinner.

Admittedly, my initial response was suspicion, but my heart softened the moment I found the letter inside. If nothing else, the gesture proved he wasn't as indifferent to our situation as he claimed to be. Inside the basket was sufficient cheese and bread for a week's worth of midnight snacks, not to mention a variety of dried fruits and my favorite chocolates from a candymaker in Revalia. He'd even included some pastries and muffins, along with an assortment of loose teas and coffee beans from one of the bakeries.

By all accounts, it was a very thoughtful bounty, not to mention expensive. I was glad nobody—namely my sister—was around to see me blushing fiercely and making excited cooing noises as I dug out one fantastic treat after another. I couldn't wait to sample everything.

It was a good apology, too. The letter was thoughtful and genuine, though I did still want to hear the words. How he'd managed to select such perfect items was beyond me. It was almost like the grumpy Gaius I thought I knew and this one, the one I worked quietly beside in his hut, were different men altogether.

A ball of heat knotted in my chest. I was hopeful. The Gaius I'd known to this point had a very difficult time admitting when he was wrong in any capacity, so I took this gesture as quite a leap in a new direction.

Invigorated by his generosity, I went around the conclave, searching huts one after another, intent on finding a chair that was wider, deeper, and much more comfortable for sitting than the one he had. I had no idea if he'd take the gesture as I meant it—a way for him to not be perpetually causing himself more discomfort—or if he'd be insulted.

For larger-sized beings, we'd certainly collected a lot of furniture that accommodated smaller human bodies instead of our own. While many dwellings boasted only cushions, nearly all of the ones that had chairs contained the skinny, straight-backed wooden abominations I was trying to replace. It took me over an hour of tromping in and out of unoccupied huts to find a single chair that I considered a decent candidate for my purposes, and another hour to decide that of the three I'd found, my first was, of course, the best option.

Slightly miffed, and already designing something better than any of them in my head, I hauled the chair to Gaius's hut. It was late, and I knocked, fully expecting to hear his footsteps grumpily thumping toward me, but it was quiet inside. I peered around the building, finding the windows were dark, as well.

My bright mood quickly turned to deep suspicion, because if he wasn't here, where was he? I had several guesses, and none of them were good.

After knocking a third time, I turned the handle and swung the door open wide. "Don't mind if I do," I muttered to myself, hauling the chair in before lighting one of the oil lamps.

After a quick look around, impressed at the progress he'd made in my absence, I installed the chair where he normally sat, moving the terrible chair to the other side of the small table. I found myself smiling, thinking of us sitting across from one another while we worked. Though, honestly, I'd much prefer the softness of the bed.

I knew I should leave quickly, I was invading his space in the worst way, but I couldn't make myself go without spending at least a few minutes with the jewelry. I sat in the newly acquired chair, pleased with my choice, as I picked one full necklace from the nearly finished bunch. Hanging it on the board of pegs before dampening the lamp, I then returned to my apartment ... with the remaining tangled nests of chains.

IT WAS BEYOND late when Gaius pounded on my door.

I'd fallen asleep on the sofa after pulling no fewer than fifteen necklaces out of one of the knots. I hadn't been waiting for him, not exactly, but the later the hour I got, the more I worried about what kind of trouble he might have gotten into. I'd decided while doing a thorough sampling of the treasures in my basket of treats that I'd likely be woken to the sound of the infirmary bell. It was rare I was so happy to be wrong.

"Lovette? Open the door." His tone betrayed annoyance, but he was also not nearly as loud as he could have been, which seemed unusually polite.

"Coming." I yawned as I crossed the room, heart pounding in anticipation of which version of the man I might find on the other side of the door.

"You took the necklaces?" he asked, worry pulling his features into stark lines.

"Yes."

His shoulders sagged in relief, but a scowl quickly formed. "I told you they were not to leave my hut."

"They're right over there. Would you like to come in?" I gestured to the low table between my two sofas.

Gaius grumbled something under his breath as he limped over, doing inventory of what I'd taken at a glance. He spun. "You brought me a different chair?"

"I did. The one you had was doing you no favors. Would you like some tea? I was gifted a lovely assortment recently." I raised an eyebrow. He was stunned into momentary silence. "Thank you for that, by the way. I love everything. The letter ... well. I appreciate it very much."

He opened his mouth and closed it again. "You're welcome. And no to the tea. What exactly are you wearing?"

I glanced down at the oversized tunic I used for sleeping and observed how it brushed my knees like an oddly designed summer dress. "A tunic? Have a seat."

"I shouldn't stay," he said, suddenly uncomfortable. "I just wanted to be sure nothing had been taken. You'll bring them back tomorrow?"

"If you like. I made some good headway tonight. I was only trying to be efficient." We both knew I was lying. I'd taken them to provoke him, left evidence it was me even. "Were you out causing trouble? Anything I should know about?"

He sat stiffly on the opposite sofa, one hand reaching to rub at his achy leg the moment he was off his feet. "Nothing noteworthy, just a visit to a tavern with ... an old friend," he said.

"Mmm." Heat bloomed in my cheeks, an unexpected flare of jealousy that took me by surprise.

Gaius rubbed at the space over his heart with the heel of his hand, the same place that was now burning in me, as well. The bond didn't care to be ignored, especially when we were in such close proximity.

"I am truly sorry, Lovette."

"Your letter was very sincere, but I appreciate you saying it, as well. I could certainly have said some things differently myself."

He looked up, gaze tortured. "You spoke the truth, nothing more. For what it's worth ... you were right." He swallowed, as though the words scratched his throat on their way out.

"That's ... Thank you."

He gave a gentle nod, and I saw it again, his exhaustion. The scent of hoppy ale and salty tavern stew lingered on his skin.

"Let me see," I said as I traded my seat for the one next to him. He stiffened as my shoulder brushed his arm. "Your leg. Let me see."

"I'm fine."

I sighed, boldly reaching out with my hand and gripping his jaw. "I'm too damn tired to argue with you, Gaius. I can tell you're hurting. Let me see your leg. Now. Please." Eyes wide, he swallowed again, turning to the side as he allowed me to pull his calf over my knees. With my fingers, I probed the tight muscles and made sure the bones and ligaments were where they should be. "You need to use your cane," I said, returning his foot to the floor.

He scowled. "It makes me look weak."

"*Not* using it will actually *make* you weak, stubborn man. It's a tool, much like your sword, nothing to be ashamed of. Didn't Imogen make it for you? Is that not enough reason to use it?"

He actually snorted a laugh. "Fair point."

"It's good for balance, support. You need it."

"Doctor's orders?" he teased, good humor sending a rush of heat through me.

"Damn right. I'm no physician, though."

"Close enough, healer. And who am I to argue with such an authority." His sigh was deep and long-suffering.

I laughed outright then, appreciating how his entire face changed when he smiled in response, becoming younger somehow. "You'd argue with me on principle, no matter what I said."

His grin widened, and my pulse sped up to the point of leaving me lightheaded. "Perhaps." His voice went breathy and low. "Maybe I like the way you fight with me, Little Dove. Not many are brave enough to face me down the way you do. It does something to me."

"Oh?" My face was on fire as he stared at me, the tension between us a thick cloud of lust and uncertainty.

I had no idea how to do ... whatever this was. Everything was new, thrilling. Terrifying. The bond smoldered hot under my ribs, my heart thumping so hard I was surprised I couldn't see it through my shirt.

"Why do you have this effect on me, Lovette? I can't think past you. You're always there, in all the places you shouldn't be. My head, my sheets. Your little tools hidden among the drawers in my armoire. Even tonight, I was with your father, of all people, and all I wanted to do was see your face. I wanted you to be proud of me for doing the right thing."

"You were with my father? He's the old friend?"

"Yes."

"What right thing were you doing?"

"We both apologized."

"You did?" I nearly squealed the words, they came out with such enthusiasm.

"The rift has been mended, I daresay. And I'm very pleased to see that look on your face for real, make no mistake. But I don't want to talk about him right now. Not after you grabbed my face like that."

"What do you want to talk about?" I asked, but my words disappeared into breath as he raised a hand, running his fingers down my cheek, across my jaw. He used his thumb to pluck at my bottom lip, his eyes slipping closed as he released a heavy breath.

"I should go," he whispered.

I said nothing and literally bit my tongue so I wouldn't beg him not to. My chest ached to the point of pain. I wanted him to touch me more. To kiss me, to seal this thing between us, to make it real.

"Tell me to go, Lovette."

"I wouldn't have invited you in if I wanted that. And I am proud of you, Gaius."

He groaned, the sound wounded and harsh. Then several things happened at once, my spinning head and pounding heart too slow to respond until it was done. His arms slid around my waist and he leaned back, which left him reclined across the sofa cushions with me astride his lap, a glazed look in his eyes and a very obvious need pulsing between us.

Especially because there was nothing under my tunic.

"**G**AIUS," I BREATHED. The ache in my chest and the sudden throb between my thighs was so intense I worried I might go mad soon. My center pressed against his hard length through his trousers, no room to spare for even the slightest bit of shame. I couldn't fathom ignoring the demands of the bond for many months if it always felt like this, let alone years.

"I shouldn't, but I just need to feel you," he said, the words a whisper against my throat. The pads of his fingers ran along my thighs, the sensitive skin on the back of my knees. "How are you so soft?"

My eyes slipped closed at the tingly sensations his touch provided. Every place his fingers brushed turned to liquid fire. I muttered something, but I didn't even know if they were real words since my mind was so scrambled. I was feverish, my eyes wouldn't focus, and my throat was dry. There was nothing I could do to slow my heartbeat down and nothing I wanted more than for him to continue the delicate torture he was putting me through.

Suddenly he stopped. I opened my eyes and focused long enough to see him frowning, his hands loosely in front of his chest as he examined them.

"My hands. Are they too rough? The callouses ..."

I shook my head. "No." Doubt creased his forehead. I reached out a hand, grasping his fingers in mine, pressing them to my cheek. "I like the way your hands feel on me."

A shuddered breath rattled through him as he stared into my eyes. After a long moment, he found whatever he'd been looking for and allowed his fingers to venture further up my body. He adjusted the way I was sitting so I was upright before moving his warm palms along my sides, then to the soft expanse of my belly. I jerked when he hit a sensitive area, and he deepened the touch, made it more intentional as he slid his fingers along the bones of my hips. I felt the rasp of his skin more intensely in the little grooves there, the ones I'd gotten the summer I grew half a foot.

His breath slid along my skin as he sat up and reversed our positions so that he was on top. My tunic became fisted in his hands as he drew it up my body and over my head, twisting it so that it knotted around my wrists. He gasped, finding I wore nothing underneath. I'd been in my own home and ready for bed, after all. "Little Dove, you are a wonder. Truly a gift." He exhaled slowly through his nose, as though grounding himself before continuing. "This leaves me one-handed for a bit, but I think that's fine, yes? I will be forced to take my time discovering every inch of you. Are you alright?" He stared down at me, eyes glassy, perhaps feeling as drunk on me as I was on his touch.

"Yes. Please."

He grumbled again, low in his chest, before devouring my mouth in a kiss that left no doubt he'd finally gotten over his worry about our differences. His lips mapped mine slowly, his tongue teasing along the seam, requesting entrance. I sighed out as the back of his fingers brushed along the side of my breast, giving him exactly what he wanted.

Gaius was like a starved man, feasting on my breath, my taste. His hand rose up to cradle my cheek, the bulk of his body pressing mine into the cushions as his fingers twisted in the shirt holding my hands above my head. The noises he made only added to the flames burning bright within my veins, and every small groan left my thighs more clenched as I sought some kind of relief from the pressure between them.

I gasped when he finally released my mouth, his lips finding my collarbone, my shoulder, the slope of my breast. "Gaius."

"Tell me to stop, Lovette." His voice was strained.

"No. Never."

He growled then, a tortured, fierce noise. He paused to breathe before he nipped a trail down my throat. His hot breath fanned along my skin, leaving me shivering. Abruptly, he grabbed me up and carried me into my bedroom, dropping me onto the mattress before caging me in with his arms, his hands on either side of my head. "That's better."

He continued his exploration at a torturously slow pace, returning my hands to their raised position above my head every time they strayed to tangle in his hair, eventually leaving one hand around both of my wrists so I had no other choice.

His body was a study in strength, every part of him made of sculpted muscle that twitched at the smallest movement. I ached to run my palms down his chest, the ripples of his stomach. I wanted to see each of the silver scars his flesh was decorated in up close and personal, taste the story of his life with my mouth.

Instead, I had to survive the blissful torture of him doing the exact same thing to me. And he was taking his sweet time about it.

"Gaius." I couldn't keep the whine out of my tone, no matter how hard I tried.

Finally, he cupped my breast in his palm, lowering his hot mouth around the peak. I made a noise that was somewhere between pain and pleasure as he sucked. Time ceased to exist as he applied the same treatment on the other side, alternating the two for what seemed like ages before eventually drifting down my body with his tongue and teeth.

"Leave those there," he warned again, taking his hand off my wrists.

"But I want to touch you too," I rasped.

"I couldn't stand it," he panted. "I'm already on the edge of my control, Lovette. If you touched me back it would be my undoing." The tremor in his voice told me he was being very, very serious.

"This time," I agreed. "But I want a turn."

He nodded enthusiastically, his long hair tickling along my skin. "Yes. Yes, Little Dove, I want that too. Just not right now."

I craved that more than anything—to see him losing control by my hand. The thought alone made my blood sing in a way I'd never felt before.

Gaius slid off the side of the mattress onto his knees. He tugged me by my ankles, sliding me right to the edge until my calves rested on his shoulders. My naked center was exposed, directly in front of his face, but instead of feeling embarrassed like I had the previous time I'd found myself in such a position, I felt powerful. The way he looked at me, the tentative way he kept kissing at whatever piece of my leg he could get to as he stroked along my thighs with his fingertips, getting closer and closer to where I wanted him ... it would feed my needy heart for weeks.

"So soft," he repeated, the words drifting off to a whisper before he inhaled deeply. "Saints. I am unworthy of this."

"You're not."

He dragged his tongue up my slit, from bottom to top, making me squirm. "I want to believe you, Little Dove." He did it again. And again. And again.

"Gaius." I exhaled with a huff, frustrated as my pulse taunted me loudly in my ears.

"Patience. I'll not be rushed. Not after all this waiting." One of his arms wrapped around my thigh, his palm pressing down on my lower belly as he latched onto where I wanted him most and sucked.

The pressure was so sudden and intense I cried out, a low guttural noise from somewhere deep within me. The fingers of his other hand gently stroked the delicate skin around my opening, teasing along the edge as I desperately tried to press myself closer to his touch. He grunted, and even without words, I knew he was admonishing me for my lack of patience, the one thing he'd requested.

"Please," I begged. Every place he touched, every inch his breath caressed burned like liquid flame. "You're the one who was in denial, don't punish *me* for it."

There was no way to know for sure, but it felt he smiled against my flesh as he dipped a finger inside me and redoubled his efforts against me with his tongue.

I writhed, lifting my hands and lowering them again, wanting to grab fistfuls of his hair but also trying to obey by leaving them over my head like he'd instructed. A slow throb built, and he curled his finger, pressing into the soft area at the front of me.

Stars filled my vision, and I knew there was no stopping the avalanche of sensation he provoked. "Gaius, I'm going to ..." Every muscle clenched as the hot knot of desire in my center finally loosened.

But he didn't stop. As I pulsed against his mouth and hand, he continued on, firmer than before. My thighs began to shake, and I couldn't stop myself from pulling my hands free of my tunic so they could tangle in his hair.

When I came back to myself, I was breathing hard and he was sitting back on his heels, a satisfied smirk on his face. "That was the prettiest thing I've ever seen, Little Dove. Let's get you some of that chocolate and maybe some tea so I can see it again."

IT WAS INDEED not my turn at all that night. That's not to say I didn't come out a winner, because I absolutely did, but my mate had taken no pleasure of my body nor allowed me to give it back to him. The bond was not fulfilled. And I honestly wasn't sure what that meant.

He was gone in the morning, which added another layer to my confusion. We'd cloistered ourselves in my apartment, but now I worried perhaps with my preference for open windows his hut would have been a better choice. Had he been unable to rest? Perhaps he'd gone somewhere to seek stone sleep instead. Or maybe he'd left because he was uncomfortable. I hated that I'd slept so soundly. It was very unlike me, and for once it would have been nice to have woken to something as innocuous as the bed shifting.

I waited around long enough to drink two cups of coffee, allowing him plenty of time to return if he'd gone to fetch breakfast. But he never showed.

Still riding enough of a hormonal high to keep from being too sour, I bathed quickly and dressed before taking myself down to the meetinghouse for a quick breakfast. To my great misfortune, my sister was there.

"Would you look at that?" she teased as she waved me over. "She lives and breathes. I haven't seen you in so long I was beginning to worry."

"It's been less than two days," I scoffed.

"Still. You're avoiding me."

"I'm not. Not anymore anyway." I sprinkled some seasoning on my eggs, bravely meeting her eye.

"If you say so." She leaned back, staring right through me as she sipped her coffee. "Where's your friend?" She raised her eyebrow.

"I have no idea. I'm not in charge of watching him." I shrugged my shoulders, trying to loosen up the sudden tension between them. I guess I wasn't as unaffected by him not being there when I woke up this morning as I'd thought.

"Mm-hmm. Fine then. What are your plans for the day?"

I shrugged, shoveling in food while I thought up a reasonable response. "I've got some things to take care of."

After the last big gathering, the one where the clan had welcomed Grace along with Calla and her mate, Rylan, as well as Greta and her mate, Vassago, I'd been left with an assortment of fabrics by the aunts. They hoarded beads and thread for our traditional gowns, but sometimes I got lucky and they'd leave me the cast-offs or bits they couldn't use elsewhere. I had some very fancy bandages at one point, in fact. The heavy canvas I'd been given would be wonderful for a chair. I just had to figure out how to get a proper frame made that lined up with my specifications, ones I'd been working on during spare moments since my hunt for a better chair for Gaius had been so unnecessarily frustrating.

"How busy are you? Can you help me with a special project, or should I go into Revalia to a smithy?"

"Get me the measurements, and I'll let you know." Imogen looked at me sideways one final time before getting to her feet. "You're not doing anything reckless, are you, Lovette?" Her grin taunted me.

"No. Should I be?"

She barked a laugh. "You probably should, actually. But I was just checking. My duty as older sister, after all."

"What about you?" I challenged. "How's Brom?" Imogen got to her feet. "Just doing my job as annoying younger sister, after all."

She left the meetinghouse without saying another word, but her lack of response and extended middle finger was enough answer for me.

When I finally got over to the infirmary, I had to reacquaint myself with the room. I stopped at the supplies cabinet, ran my fingers over the tools, checked on the stores of alcohol and medicines. I felt oddly distanced from it, and I wasn't sure what that meant.

After finding the fabric, my shears, and a measuring tape, I remembered that while fine stitchwork on wounds was my specialty, I was no seamstress. While the concept I'd thought up was fairly simple, the execution was anything but. It turned out it didn't matter, however, because I'd barely had time to get my initial measurements made before a cluster of young gargoyles came crashing through the open doorway.

"Healer! We've got injured!"

Four of them carried two men between them, a trail of blood staining the floor as they traipsed through and dumped their cargo on my cots.

Heart pounding, I abandoned my project and peered into the face of the first man, shocked to my core at who I found.

CHAPTER 14
GAIUS

"BY ALL THE saints, what are *they* doing here? And why are they bleeding so much?" Lovette demanded, voice raised as she pushed the soldiers out of her way and began to gather supplies.

"I should think it obvious, daughter, that they're here *because* they are bleeding." Magnus wore a grin. He'd enjoyed our early questioning of this pair as much or more than I had.

She clucked her tongue at him, hands full of bandages. "Fine. But my question still stands. It is rare that council members leave the council building, is it not? Why are they utilizing the conclave for healing instead of their own infirmary?"

"Ah, well, that would be due to the fact that we abducted them for questioning," he answered. "Their answers were not overwhelmingly forthcoming so ..." Magnus pulled a face, gesturing with his hands as though their current state explained everything his words didn't. "Besides, it wasn't just us. We stopped at d'Arcan on the way so our friends and relations could clear up some things with them as well." He gestured to some marks on both of the councilmen's clothing. "It's Rylan's fault they smell of scorch."

I hadn't realized how unhinged my old friend could be until today. I'd seen one of the demons in action against the hordes, but I had a new appreciation for them both after witnessing firsthand the grace and technique they used to encourage Hugo and Augustus to talk. My mistrust in them simply because they were demons had faded to nearly nothing, and I was grateful to have them as allies.

Lovette gaped back at him, her mouth open and eyes blinking slowly. "Honestly," she swore, shaking her head.

"Help them so they can heal up properly in stone sleep, if you can, Little Dove." Her eyes flicked to me, and my skin warmed as I realized the endearment had slipped out.

"Of course I can," she said indignantly. Then she ordered the soldiers who hovered by the beds watching our conversation with amusement to move Hugo and Augustus to her liking. I didn't bother to stifle my smile when they groaned out as their idea of "properly positioned to receive medical care" was proven to be vastly different than hers.

"You'll face trial for this, the both of you!" Augustus choked out, groaning as Lovette packed a sizable wound in his abdomen with gauze and wrapped him with a wide bandage.

"Unlikely," I said, crossing my arms as I settled in to watch her work. "I'm fairly certain the other council members will have plenty of questions for you as well once we present our findings."

"Findings?" Lovette asked, moving on to treating Hugo.

"I'm very much looking forward to confirming my suspicions about several things. Let's leave it at that for now," Magnus said.

Lovette focused on her father's face. "The ... What you've been searching for?"

He smiled broadly, a mix of satisfaction and relief on his face. I wasn't sure what she was referring to, but with Magnus looking like that, I guessed it was important.

"Yes. I hope so."

Lovette smiled back. "How wonderful." She turned to Hugo. "Stop moving, and it won't be quite as painful." She shifted him around once again, making him grunt, which brought me a special kind of joy. I was usually on the receiving end of her forcible ministrations, and it was nice to see I hadn't been given special treatment.

"What are you dosing the guards with?" I asked, realizing we'd never gotten around to that during the time we'd been with the demons. We'd covered plenty else, but that detail had been left out. "To make them not remember?"

Hugo gasped, and Augustus choked on a laugh. "What a ridiculous question."

"Is it?" I stepped forward, into the space between their beds. Lovette moved to the far side of Hugo's bed and Magnus to Augustus's. "How long?" I asked, catching the glance they shared. "How. Long." I pressed my palm into the open wound Lovette had just dressed in Augustus's abdomen.

He gasped, trying in vain to push my hand away. Magnus frowned deeply.

The new shift of soldiers came in just as Magnus applied a similar pressure to Hugo, repeating the question of what, precisely, they were giving to whom and under what direction.

"I'll get more bandages, then." Lovette gave a soft huff as she returned to the cabinet, dispersing three younger stone kin sentries who stood before it throughout the room.

One at a time, the councilmen flinched as Lovette pressed a hand to their bodies while she worked to undo the damage we'd inflicted. It was obvious the moment her unique talent of stealing anxiety from someone worked its magic on them. I hated that they got such a gift. They didn't deserve it.

"Speak!" Magnus demanded.

"May I?" Lovette asked.

"Be my guest." Magnus stepped back, and Lovette sat next to Augustus on the narrow cot.

"Councilman, have you been giving loyal stone kin a potion of some kind? Something that would make them not remember things?" He turned ashen as her nimble fingers began the delicate stitchwork she was so skilled at one-handed, pulling nearly invisible thread through the skin along his stomach. Her other hand forcefully pressed the edges of the wound together, narrowing the gap. "Think carefully before you answer."

"I don't know what you're—" The movement of her arm was barely perceptible, but Augustus jerked. Then he shrieked, and everyone in the room tensed. Lovette glanced up at me, oddly vacant eyes focused on my face as she removed the fingers she'd sunk into his open wound, wiping them on her apron. She turned away again, making him yell out once more a she pulled out the stitch he'd fouled by twitching.

I'd rarely seen this Lovette when I'd needed care. Though when I had, I'd likely deserved it. She was nothing short of terrifying. Even her father looked as though he'd prefer to leave rather than watch her work when she became this cold, distant version of herself, not to mention the soldiers behind us.

"Would you like to try again? I didn't hear you. I'm afraid it's terribly important to know." Her hands began moving again.

"How could you? What about your oath? Haven't you sworn to do no harm?"

Lovette barked a short laugh, the sound edged in darkness. The tiny hairs on my neck prickled at the sound. "No harm? You were there the night I killed those guards, were you not? They were threatening us, so I had no choice, of course. Still, you saw it happen."

"That's not ... this is different. I'm in your care. You're not supposed to—"

"I've taken no such oath, councilman. I'm not a physician. Only an exceptionally well-trained healer." My eyes widened as her arm jerked and he cried out again. "Now, if you wouldn't mind answering my question, I would appreciate it very much."

Hugo was panting and sweating as he watched his friend get sewn up. "Oh, for saint's sake, Auggie. It's not worth—"

"Quiet, Hugo!"

She tutted her tongue, using her teeth to break the thread. "Seems I worked a bit too efficiently. That's too bad. Hugo? Would you mind sharing what you know? I'd hate to see that fester. Some things not even stone sleep can cure. Would be a fascinating thing to study, though."

As Lovette reached for a bottle of antiseptic, Hugo sputtered, his hands up in a defensive position. "It's a tonic. I don't know how it's made or from what—that's none of my concern. The witch council provides it."

My blood turned to lava. "How long?" I demanded.

"As long as I've been in my seat. Longer. I don't know!"

"Shut up, Hugo!" Augustus complained, but Magnus stepping closer was all it took for him to quiet down.

"Can the effects be reversed?"

"I don't know."

Lovette stitched as fast as she dared, her jaw ticking in concentration.

By the time we knew where in the council building to find records of the tonic and perhaps even a sample, she'd done enough to ensure they would recover, then we were left with two grimacing statues on the cots after Magnus forced them into stone sleep.

Lovette washed her hands thoroughly, scrubbing at her fingernails as the soldiers took their leave at Magnus's request. There would be another shift coming in soon enough, and neither councilman was leaving while frozen as a statue.

"The missing?" Lovette asked Magnus in a voice barely above a whisper, drying her hands on a worn towel. Exhaustion lined her face, but there was a light in her eyes indicating she'd returned to herself.

"A very solid lead." He grinned again, tracking her as she moved around the room, setting supplies to rights and cleaning up. She hugged him, no words needed for them to share their matching emotion about such a thing. "I'll retrieve the tonic. Perhaps Greta can work it backwards to find out what it is, how to reverse the memory loss."

The roiling pit in my gut settled slightly. I was terrified at what I might have forgotten over the years, but having The Alchemist back with the stone kin, there was at least a partial chance of remembering. Though I wasn't sure that was something I wanted to do either; I could very well lose everything.

Magnus excused himself to get some supper at the meeting-house, leaving us alone. I fidgeted, eventually frustrated with myself enough that I sat on the edge of a cot so I would stop moving.

"You feeling alright?" she asked.

"No worse than usual," I sighed. "You?" I desperately wanted to pull her to my chest, to comfort her. Whatever happened when she went to that cold place, I didn't care for, and I was sure it had lingering effects on her too.

"I'm fine." She gave a weak smile as she returned to tidying up. It was comforting, her very methodical work. The replacement sentries arrived just as she finished, taking their places with a quiet nod.

"Come on," she said, leading me out. "Food. Then rest." She turned her face to the sky once we were outside, taking a deep breath. "Go on back to your hut. I'll be along shortly."

I didn't argue, just started down the path, my leg throbbing with every step, my arm sore and buzzing with a strange electrical current.

Words were few when she arrived with the basket. We ate in silence, and she packed everything except our mugs of ale away once we were finished. I hadn't even realized I was massaging my forearm until she reached for my hand.

"Let me help you, Gaius," she said, steel in her eyes.

My chest began to ache as much as my limbs. Besides, when she said it like that, what option did I have? I placed my arm on the tabletop, and she drew it down into her lap, golden hair falling into her face as she began to work. I closed my eyes, grateful for the peace her touch brought, even if I was certain I didn't deserve the mercy.

CHAPTER 14
LOVETTE

"YOU SHOULD BE getting regular massages like this, you
know. Therapy for the tissue if it bothers you so much."

"I'm fine."

I sighed deeply, probing at the scar between the two areas of
his forearm with my fingertips. "You are many things, Gaius
Caledon. Fine is not one of them." He grunted, but when I looked
up, his eyes had slipped halfway closed. "Are you going to argue
with me all night? We both know you need this."

His face went through several fascinating changes through the
span of several breaths. Finally, he sighed. "Do your worst, healer."

His capitulation was music to my ears. "You sure? You've quite
recently seen my worst." I knew I'd done nothing wrong today ...
but I hated who I became sometimes out of necessity.

I got up to get a bottle of heavy ointment that Greta had sent
over with my father, his empathetic gaze following me. She'd
prepared a lotion with a new Elixir of Healing mixed into it. My
cousin was an alchemist and had fully embraced her calling at
d'Arcan. The little box she'd sent with Father contained no fewer

than a dozen little vials, all magical in their own way, all a boon for us to have.

After warming the balm between my hands, I massaged it into the skin all around the joint, using one hand to balance his forearm while rubbing small circles over the scar with the fingertips of the other.

His fingertips flexed and relaxed as I worked over the strong muscles on the underside of his forearm. I was amused watching the mechanics work as they should. "Nerves and reflexes all seem in order."

"Mmm." His eyes blinked heavily, the relaxation evident in his slower breathing.

I failed to stifle the smile his response gave me, the corners of my mouth lifting gently as he sank further into his seat as I worked.

I reached for his ankle once the balm had all been absorbed on his arm. He shifted his foot away from my grasp. "Does your arm feel better?"

He frowned. "Yes."

"Then let me also do your leg." Gaius heaved a sigh, as I pulled his calf over my knees. I simply glared back. His discontent quickly turned into a low rumbling groan of happiness as I worked the ointment into the knotted flesh. He was a melted puddle of a man, eyes closed and mouth slack, when I finally finished and returned his foot to the floor.

"Why do you fight it so when you know it will help? We've been through this." I chuckled, shaking my head.

"Because I don't deserve relief," he said after a moment.

"Ridiculous. You are not required to pay penance for the rest of your days in the form of discomfort, Gaius."

"You sure, Little Dove?" I was pinned by the misery in his stare. "I've done things I can never atone for. Seems a constant reminder is the least of what I deserve."

I scoffed. "This again? Get over yourself, General."

"Pardon me?" He scowled again, looking at me as though he didn't recognize me.

"You heard me. Your former behavior and past crimes don't make you special, Gaius. I would wager every solider here—plus all the ones stationed at the military outpost and the men at the *work camp* for saint's sake—have a similar story. Your self-imposed misery does nothing but keep you from healing in every way."

"You have no idea—"

"Sure I do. I've heard my father's stories, my mother's, my siblings'. Those of every injured stone kin to come through my infirmary or the meetinghouse needing to share their tales over supper. Do you think me pure? Without any stains of past deeds? You were *there* when I killed those guards."

"They were threatening you—"

"And *you*. You were there earlier today when I ..." My blood ran hot, the ache of the bond in my chest tightening and giving a dull throb. "Whatever it is you think you've done, you must forgive yourself. If needs must, list everything out on paper so I can see it all clearly and make my own choice."

"And if I can't? If I can't forgive nor forget?"

"Then you are doomed to be nothing more than a miserable old man, stuck in the past for all of eternity. Is that what you want? When you can be so much more? When you *are* so much more? You deserve better than that. I do, too, as your mate. I truly thought we'd moved past much of this."

"In one thing, we agree, Lovette. You deserve better." He bit the words out, as if my statement had confirmed what he'd already told me. A chasm began to open between us again, and I couldn't stand the idea of having to either close or cross it once more.

"Then *be more*, Gaius." Frustrated, I got to my feet and started packing up the supplies. I was not interested in rehashing this, yet again, not after what we'd already been through together.

"I do not know how, Little Dove." The quiet tone of his voice, the resignation in it and the sadness made me stop. It made my heart ache and my breath catch.

"You do too, you foolish man." I exhaled a long breath, staring into his eyes. "You have been, each day I've sat here with you and sorted jewels. Every time you've thought of someone else over your revenge."

He shook his head. "I don't. I'm not good like you, Lovette."

"Good and bad are just—"

"I don't know how to be what you *need*." His hasty interruption tapered into a deep sigh. "You are everything I lack, and it just comes naturally. I do not understand why the fates have smiled on me so, despite how I begged and tried to wheedle my way into such a blessing." He grimaced then, as though tasting something bad. "Especially because I tried to do that."

"What is it you need, Gaius?" I asked, unable to keep the words from spilling over my lips, even if they would damn me to living in a state of endless longing or regret.

He shook his head. "Just you. You are my peace, Little Dove. Your presence, your touch brings me more calm than I can ever remember having."

"It takes away the edge of anxiety perhaps, but my gift doesn't relieve pain. What's the point in it if it doesn't do that?" Frustrated by the storm of emotions swirling within me, I tugged at my shirt as I sat heavily in the chair and looked away.

His eyebrows drew together, and he leaned forward, putting his hands on either side of my face and forcing me to look into his eyes.

"The pain I can handle, Lovette. It is an annoyance, nothing more. The disquiet that has invaded my soul since I took that damnable post with the council is a constant gnawing ache driving me to madness. That doesn't even count all the years before, the anger that festered and the misguided hatred over things that, you're right, I should have learned how to move past. Moments of peace without any of that, a chance to catch my breath and get some clarity on my own mind are priceless. Your presence is a *blessing*." He slanted his mouth over mine, the kiss straightforward but potent. His hands left my face and slid around my body. I sank into his warmth as his arms tightened around me, and a lump of emotion clogged my throat. "Do not discount your value or the power of your gift." The words rumbled against my ear.

My chest glowed with the praise, the acknowledgement. I had always viewed my gift as incomplete, like the universe had forgotten to give me the other half of it. Guilt was always there when I'd be helping a patient, someone wounded and hurting, and the best I could do was to remove the anxiety of the situation instead of relieving the actual source of their pain.

Gaius's words soothed the parts of me that always ached to do more in those situations. They reminded me that sometimes the best aspects of our gifts, of ourselves, are the ones we think are missing.

"Thank you."

"Mmm," he grumbled again, tugging at the ends of my hair with his fingertips. Pulling some of the curls out straight, he then let them bounce up again. His chair scraped the floor as he scooted as close to me as possible, his arms winding around my middle, his face tucked into the curve of my neck.

I shivered as his mouth began to lay light kisses along my skin, the bond expanding under my ribs, feeling like unfiltered sunlight trying to escape the confines of my body. "Gaius."

His broad, warm palms took the measure of me in a slow, methodical way, mapping every inch of my torso and back before lowering to my thighs. His touch was firm and intentional as he replicated the massage I'd given him. One at a time, he drew my feet into his lap, working his strong thumbs into my instep, cracking the tense joints in my toes. I arched my back into the chair, unsure whether I was enjoying the sensations or not.

"You are tense, Little Dove."

"Always," I answered, sighing as he moved on to my ankles and calves.

"I wouldn't have thought so," he said. "Before."

"Before?" I nearly moaned as he released the stress from the muscle along the back of my thigh.

"Before I realized how much you carry around. For you, your family. Me. If I'm to let go of my past, you need to learn to let go of your need to think about everyone before yourself."

I made a noise of agreement, but my thoughts were already melted, especially because his wicked fingers had pulled me to the very edge of my seat. My feet touched the back of his chair, my rear barely hanging on to the edge of my seat.

"Lovette."

"Mmm?"

"I'm going to take you to my bed. If you object to this, speak your piece. Otherwise, I'm going to claim you as my mate, once and for all. You will be mine, and I will be yours, until the fates see fit to call us to the great beyond. If you don't want that, now is the time to say so." There were shadows in his eyes. Fear that I was going to say no, even still.

I found I could no longer breathe. "Yes, Gaius. I want that."

"Praise the saints and devils alike, and let them all forgive me for being selfish when it comes to you," he sighed as he scooped me up.

My legs locked around his waist as he stood with me in his arms. It was a stilted walk to the bed, but he got us there without incident. Leaning over, he pressed me into the mattress as he nipped at my mouth, teasing me with kisses that were neither long enough nor deep enough for my liking.

"What if I had said no?" I whispered, making sure there was a teasing tone to my words, a soft lift to my smile.

"I am not above begging," he smirked, fingertips grazing the sensitive tips of my breasts as they traveled the length of my torso. "I might not deserve you, Little Dove, but I sure as hell want you. I'm too far gone to let go of you now. I would have gotten on my knees every single day for the rest of eternity and pleaded with each and every deity individually, as long as it meant I got to keep you." He kissed me again, stealing my very breath with the passion he infused into those words.

"Good thing I was never going to say anything but yes, then," I panted. "I spared both your knees and your pride."

He coughed a rough laugh. "You left your scent in my sheets," he complained, but there was no fire to his accusations. "I couldn't sleep with your smell all around me. I had to stone sleep or go without rest."

His hands pushed my skirts put to my waist and pulled my undergarments down my thighs. I unlocked my ankles so he could remove them completely and sat up, reaching for the lashings on his trousers. "I'm not apologizing. And I still haven't gotten a turn."

He pushed my hands away gently. "And you still aren't getting one, Little Dove. I wouldn't last a moment. I'm already only existing on the thinnest thread of control where you're concerned."

I cared about nothing the moment his heated skin was on mine. His mouth removed any lingering thought as it worked mine with pure need. There was nothing but desire there, an ache that echoed behind my ribs as a hot, hollow throb. Clothing littered the floor, the bedding crumpled beneath my back as he ran his hand up the length of my thigh.

"I don't know if I can—"

"I'm not making requests or demands, Gaius. I need you. However you're ready to give of yourself, I'll take it." He shuddered, pressing his thumb against my folds and finding me already wet. He circled my clit as his hot length notched against me. "No going back." My tone was light, but the last thing I wanted was for him to change his mind or regret or resent this down the line.

"Never. You will be my peace for eternity, Little Dove. And I will do my best to be yours." He grunted as he surged forward, my body accepting him readily but not without a pinching, stretching sensation that made me moan. "Lovette?" he asked, panting into the curve of my neck.

"I'm fine." To prove it, I canted my hips upward, forcing him deeper. He swore an incoherent word, his breath hot against my skin.

As he slowly began to move, the mate bond expanded inside my chest like a star preparing to explode. I clawed at his chest with my fingernails, leaving behind faint red streaks over the place I imagined his bond would be. He flattened my hand under his, pressing my palm against the beat of his heart as he increased his tempo. Everywhere his skin met mine left behind a sharp tingle as an ache began to grow deep in my gut. Need and satisfaction warred, the bond growing impossibly large as my pleasure followed right behind.

My hips lifted to meet his thrusts, his one hand holding mine over his heart and the other squeezing my thigh where it rested against his hip.

"Lovette, I cannot—" His head fell back, the ends of his long hair brushing against my ankle, his throat bared to me. His Adam's apple bobbed as he swallowed, the moan he let out as his rhythm became erratic pushing me over the edge.

My own wordless cry seemed to assuage his worry. My body clenched around his as the bond expanded so far it had to have gone beyond the bounds of my flesh. Gaius surged forward one final time, collapsing over the top of me in a flurry of kisses pressed to my face, my chest, my shoulders.

"Mine," he declared, our hands trapped between us.

His pulse raced under my hand, the beat the same frantic one as mine. All at once, the heat and pressure of the bond disappeared, leaving behind what felt like a thread between us. It gave a gentle pull as Gaius carried me to the bathroom and lavished me with a thorough wash under the spray of the shower.

After, as we lay in his bed together under the sheets, my head propped on his chest and his arms around me, a chill crept through me. It was a rude interruption to the warm, peaceful bubble I was in.

"We have to tell everyone soon," I whispered. No matter how sure I was that it would all be fine, a creeping doubt that there would be objections to our coupling dampened my joy.

Our relationship had only been ours to this point. There was speculation, sure, but we'd had a tiny, insulated world inside this hut for ourselves. And that was over now. There was no going back.

Gaius sighed, the depth of it echoing the worry I carried. He kissed my temple. "I know, Little Dove. We will. Soon."

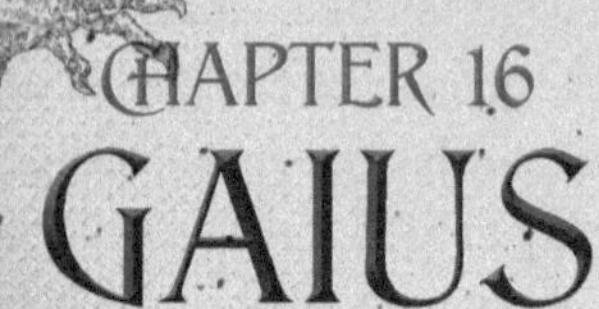

CHAPTER 16
GAIUS

"S OON" CAME WITH the sunrise.

It was early, and we were focused on one another as we left her apartment instead of our surroundings. I had my hand at the small of Lovette's back as we walked, my cane assisting with the trek per her nonnegotiable orders. I'd leaned in close to whisper one of my intentions for our time alone later on. It made her blush and blurt a laugh just as Magnus and Imogen came around the edge of the building together.

"Oh! Good morning," Lovette greeted them, the hand that she'd placed on my arm dropping slowly to her side. "I was just about to check on the patients."

Magnus's gaze traveled between us, surprise and something darker flashing in his eyes. Imogen seemed to be bracing for her father's response more than anything, which I understood. She'd been the one to give me the gift suggestions, after all, so she clearly knew there was something between us.

"Good morning, Lovette, Gaius." Magnus's eyebrows drew

together. "No need, the councilmen have been transported back to d'Arcan for further detainment."

"The collegium? Not the camp?" Lovette asked, shifting her weight from one foot to the other under her father's stare. "Were they healed enough to travel after stone sleeping?"

"Yes, they were perfectly well, the lucky bastards. We've invited the archmage and his brother to serve as neutral parties for their imprisonment while the council decides next steps. The labor camp seemed a bit too aggressive to the council and the outpost too high risk as far as a possible unknown ally on the inside."

"Seems wise." I nodded.

"Did you already eat breakfast?" Lovette asked.

"Just finished," Imogen answered. "If you hurry, the bread will still be warm."

Magnus crossed his arms, widening his stance as he did so. I recognized the posture, and my blood rose in response, needing nothing further to prepare to defend my mate. Lovette saw it as well and patted my arm in much the same way Imogen reached out to grip her father's shoulder.

"Is there ... a *we* between the two of you?" Magnus asked, his attention focused on Lovette. I wasn't sure if he was covering rage, disgust, or some other emotion, or if he was truly just asking a question. Either way, I didn't care for the tone he used. It made the bond flare to angry life, and made every little hair on my body standing straight up.

"Don't do that," I gritted out.

"Sorry? Do what, exactly?" Magnus's head tilted a bit as his eyes shifted between me and his daughter.

"There's no reason to speak to her that way, General."

His frown deepened. "What way is that, Gaius?"

"Like you're accusing her of something sordid."

"I did no such thing."

"Hey," Lovette interrupted, one arm out to each of us, as though interrupting a fight that hadn't yet begun. "There's no need for this, truly."

"I'm just asking if my daughter has become romantically involved with someone. A man I believed to be a friend. This isn't some ploy, is it, Gaius? I believed your apologies were genuine at the Empty Cask. Were they? Or were there ulterior motives at play?" He scowled, eyebrows drawn together and mouth a firm line.

"They were genuine, and nothing about our friendship has changed as far as I'm concerned. But you will not speak to or about my mate in a disparaging way, Magnus. Not even if she is your daughter. I won't allow it. She's mine and I will protect her, even from you."

"I have not spoken to her in *any* kind of way." He paused, staring me down while he considered the whole of what I'd said. "Lovette?"

"I appreciate the gesture, but I can handle my father on my own," she told me, warning in her eyes. "You heard right, Father. Gaius is my mate." She said the words plainly, her shoulders back and head held high. There was no shame in them, no fear. I was awed by her beauty and confidence in that moment, like so many others. My bond burned under my ribs, pride inflating my chest with her bold claim.

"Mates," Magnus said, slightly breathless. Imogen blew out a breath as though she too had been nervously awaiting this moment.

My instinct to lash out was too strong. I found offense where there might not be any, in an effort to protect myself. I bit out, "Am I not allowed to have even one, General? You've been gifted two after all. Do you begrudge the rest of us from finding what you have?"

"Of course I don't, Gaius." He frowned, hurt in his voice. He relaxed his stance. "Are you comfortable with this match, Lovette?"

"It poses some challenges, as most relationships do," she said, grinning at me, "but I am well satisfied with who the fates have chosen for me."

"I see."

"I did what I could to deny the bond existed when I first figured it out, for what little it was worth," I stated, realizing too late my words might wound Lovette. "This wasn't intentional."

"The best and worst things in life never are." Magnus's mouth curled into a weak smile.

"He was prepared to go mad for me." Lovette shrugged, as though that explained it all. I appreciated that she didn't mention my offer to die for her. That seemed a bit much, all things considered, true or not.

Magnus looked between us several times, his posture relaxing further each time his eyes moved from her to me and back again. "I am happy for you, if you are glad of the match. Both of you. I can't think of two people more deserving of the joy a true mate can bring."

I scowled at him, trying to detect the deception I was sure was there under his kind words. Lovette, on the other hand, bounced up on her toes, pulling away from me to throw her arms around her father's neck.

"I told him that's how you would feel."

Magnus stared at me over his daughter's shoulder, no doubt taking stock of his unexpected new relation. "Many pairings are … unconventional. My own included. Who am I to argue with the fates?" he asked, though it sounded a little like he wanted to do just that. "Gaius, we need to have a discussion later—unrelated to this, of course."

"What about?" I bristled.

"We seem to be lacking proper training staff at the outpost at the moment. Too many men retiring out and not enough with the skills to replace them. I thought perhaps, you might find a good fit there."

My stomach clenched. "I don't need a pity post, Magnus."

He clucked his tongue at me, as though I were a confused youngling. "This is anything but, I assure you. The only men left manning the training academy sector of the military outpost here in Revalia are Woldrop and Prater." I unintentionally made a face. "Precisely." Magnus sighed.

"What about Rumford and Bogan? Jennor?"

"All retired, along with a handful of others from the ranks. It's been quite a year." Magnus sighed again, looking tired. How he kept everything organized like he did wore me out on his behalf. I'd been more than happy to stick to my little corner of the city, with my men and my responsibilities.

"Alright. I suppose it wouldn't hurt to listen."

"Wonderful. I'll catch up with you this evening then. Meetinghouse?"

"Yes, I'll come meet you."

"Father, before you go, how do you feel about Brom?" Lovette chirped.

Magnus frowned, thoughtful. "The leathersmith's apprentice? I don't know, seems nice enough. Wasn't he in your brother's class? Why?"

Imogen threw a glare that should have incinerated Lovette where she stood but only seemed to provide her with amusement before giving her father's arm one final pat. Then she took a step away from our gathering. "Congratulations, the pair of you." She threw another deadly look at Lovette before turning her attention to her father. "*I'm* going to tend my furnace." She gestured back to us. "*They* are going to go eat some breakfast, and *you* are going to check in with the archmage, yes?"

"Yes, that's—" Magnus started, but Imogen wasn't done.

"Also, Ophelia invited you to visit if you needed some encouragement with these new developments, though you're taking this all rather well, I think."

"Ophelia?" we asked her in chorus, which made Lovette's mouth twitch in amusement while mine tightened.

"When did you see Ophelia?" Magnus asked, the notion that they'd gone to the ancient sorceress now clearly his primary concern, and I could relate. She was a terrifyingly unpredictable woman.

"Not long ago. She sends her regards and extended an invitation to visit should you need some ... clarity on the subject of mate bonds. I hear she's very fond of salted licorice."

"Yes, I'm aware," he mumbled, following behind her as her long legs carried her toward the forge.

When I turned from watching them walk away, adrenaline still pumping through my blood, I found Lovette smiling at me. "Come on, I'm starving."

"Is he being genuine?" I asked. Left with no choice, I followed as she tugged me down the path toward the meetinghouse doors.

"Of course he is. Have you ever known him to be false?" As we loaded up our plates and took seats across from one another for the first time in full view of our kin, I realized I never had. Magnus was honest to a fault and good natured. My interpretation of his responses were a reflection of me, not of him. And the opportunity to train the next batch of stone kin youth into efficient soldiers did hold a certain appeal.

I felt knots of tension release from my shoulders as Lovette covered my hand with hers. There were eyes on us, I could feel them, but she didn't care. I straightened, deciding that if she was unbothered, I could be too. Besides, I never wanted her to think I was anything less than proud to be seen with her.

"I'm sorry for what I said about trying to deny the bond—"

"Stop worrying about it. I wasn't offended. Just be happy, Gaius." Her joy translated directly through the way she held herself proudly, the way she smiled. The glow in my chest where our bond connected us. She was not afraid nor ashamed of what anyone in the meetinghouse had to say now that her father knew.

As we ate, her hand remained where it was, thumb gently stroking along the back of my hand. I appreciated the grounding it provided, the quiet in my head her touch always gave.

When we stood to leave, I caught the eye of several kin on our way to the door, my cane an additional thump on the wood floor as we went. They all gave a polite nod, a smile, or both.

Approval. Congratulations. Community.

I needed it all much more than they knew. And once again, I had a bold, golden-haired healer to thank for it.

CHAPTER 17
LOVETTE

I WASN'T PRIVY TO everything that happened once the coun-cilmen left my care, but I understood well that the next several months were going to be full of serious changes.

Hugo's and Augustus's fate would be decided following an investigation from within not only the stone kin council but those of the mages and witches as well. To get all of the factions involved spoke of serious transgressions ... and rumor had it they were not the only ones under a watchful eye. My father had never been so enthusiastic about being a required participant in council meetings.

Ophelia, who had yet to be wrong about much of anything, certainly had the right of things when she proclaimed it was time for the stone kin to experience change starting at the very top and to set down some roots. Construction was beginning both at d'Arcan and at the conclave, and it felt like the first breath of spring when the flowers begin to show through the soil, despite it being nearly time to turn over the earth for winter. Something good was coming. Something hopeful.

As I entered the infirmary under the cool white light of a full moon, I found it bustling with people. The cots had all been pushed against the walls to make both useful flat surfaces and more standing room.

Gaius spotted me and came over as quickly as he could, his cane thumping along the stone floor. When he kissed me on the cheek, I looked up to find my father watching, expression indiscernible. When I met his eye, though, he winked reassuringly back at me.

"Does everyone have their assignments already?" I asked, stunned at how many stone kin they'd recruited for our late-night journey into Revalia.

"Yes. Here's yours." He handed me a small grouping of necklaces hung on a short rod, each tagged with a name and address.

We'd finished sorting the jewelry just a couple of nights prior, and after enlisting some invaluable help from Calla, Grace, Greta, and the girls that worked at d'Arcan, as many items as possible had been linked to updated family names and addresses. It had taken some firm handling, but I'd managed to convince my mate that trying to manage the return of such a vast number of pieces was far more than he could handle alone, even with my help. People would start talking, and the more times we had to return, the more dangerous it would become. So, over several tankards of ale between Gaius, Imogen, and my father, a blitz was planned.

Funny thing was, the more they talked about it, thinking they were being quiet, or at least well ignored, the more people volunteered to help.

Pride swirled through me, making my heart thump and the bond glow. I looked around to find my sister mixed in the crowd, double-checking everyone had what they needed. But there was also an unfamiliar face. A demon, if I had to guess.

"Who's that?"

"Ah! Seir? If you please?" Father gestured him over. "I'd like to introduce you to my daughter."

Like his brothers, the demon was tall, quick to smile and more handsome than he had any right to be. He had short auburn hair, cut to just above his jaw, the front pieces pulled back away from his face with a leather tie. Twisted brown horns extended out and back from the top of his head through his russet hair, and he had a pair of dark wings tucked tight to his back.

Gaius shifted beside me, a frown on his face as the demon enthusiastically shook my hand. "Hello, I'm Seir."

"Lovette."

He turned to my father. "Have you installed the portal then?"

"Portal?" I asked, glancing between them.

"Like a doorway, you just need to think of where or who you want to go to and it will take you there."

"Yes, I'm aware of what they are, I just didn't know we had one of those."

"Of course you do! I gave him one ages ago."

I tilted my head, silently questioning my father. "It wasn't *that* long ago, and it's a permanent installation, I had to be sure of my choice." He shrugged.

Seir laughed, then his face abruptly became serious, and he nodded. "He's right though, once put up they cannot be moved. It's wise to be very, very sure."

"It's nice to meet you, Seir,"

"And you!" He jiggled my arm up and down once more, grinning broadly, his several additional pointed teeth showcased by the gesture. "This is going to be fun."

"Quiet down!" my father shouted. "Everyone has been briefed of the plan, correct?"

"Yes sir!" was the majority response.

"We are to move as quickly and stealthily as possible. Your entry points are on your documents. Think of that place and *only* that place as you step through the doorway. It may feel a little disorienting but having a way to move in and out faster than we could fly is very important, understood?"

"Yes sir!"

"You have one hour to deliver your items. If for some reason, it is unsafe to leave one, move on to the next. The return portal is located on the grounds at d'Arcan. Enter at the observatory, and they will direct you from there. If you have items left when the hour is up, deliver them back here. Everyone is to check in at the meetinghouse once they are finished, clear?"

"Yes sir!"

I found myself giving the response as well, adrenaline pumping as Gaius squeezed my hand, then moved to the front of the pack to lead the group out of the infirmary with my father.

We crossed the square in front of the meetinghouse, proceeding toward the ancient tree under which celebrations were always held.

"If you don't mind demonstrating?" Father asked Seir, who was positively giddy.

"Of course." With another broad grin and an odd salute to the crowd of gathered stone kin, Seir stepped up to the trunk of the tree and ... disappeared.

Several men gasped, jostling one another in jest that they would throw one another in.

"Oh, for saints' sake." I shook my head and reached for Gaius's hand. "Ready?"

"Not a chance, Little Dove, but I'll go with you anyway." He dipped down and kissed me, and then, together, we walked into the tree. For several long moments, I felt as though I was being turned inside out and upside down ... then we walked out through the smithy in the Barrens.

Gaius and I worked together, crisscrossing our area of the city in flashes of wings and moonlight. There were more stone-kin prancing across roofs, in the sky, and running around stealthily on foot than I'd ever seen in Revalia, let alone at one time.

Seir caught up to us just after we'd delivered my final necklace to a bronze letterbox. My father had also joined up with us, a broad smile on his face. Everyone was doing their job, but also having an immense amount of fun.

"It's like Samhain," Seir said with a grin, "except instead of children asking for treats, we're delivering things. Oh! Or Yule! My brothers and I always tried to sneak around late at night to leave one another little treats when we were young. We'd always end up running into one another then just sitting around in the hallway opening them. Too tempting to wait until morning."

"Demons celebrate holidays in such a manner?" Gaius asked.

"Of course we do!" Seir replied, shaking his head and waving a hand like Gaius was jesting. "Don't stone kin?" Then he disappeared.

"Wait. Did you ...?"

"I saw it too. Or rather, I didn't see where he went."

"He does that," Father said. "Instant travel, portals or otherwise, is one of his powers."

"Wouldn't that be nice?" Gaius chuffed.

When the hour was up, we flew back to the conclave, finding a full-blown party underway at the meetinghouse. If there was one thing for certain, stone kin would take any opportunity for a celebration, even during hours better served by sleeping. I hoped nobody required my attention in the infirmary because of it.

As we walked past, several of the men made a point to thank Gaius for having them along for the fun, his shoulder was sure to be sore after all the thumping. I stepped to the side and let him have a moment, his gruff expression breaking into a smile as he shook hands, trying to sidestep away from the crowd so he could follow me.

I checked in with the aunts who had been left to collect any undeliverable pieces, and Gaius finally caught up as I reached the end of the infirmary building, only a handful of leftover items in my pocket.

"Your place or mine?" he asked.

"Presumptuous question, sir."

His smile was becoming easier to tease out. "Is it? Is it presumption to ask where my mate is going to allow me the honor of enjoying her company after such a productive night's work?"

"It probably is." I threaded my fingers through his and led him toward his hut, the stairs to my apartment feeling somehow like more work than the extra walk to his door. "But I don't mind."

He snorted, squeezing my hand tightly. "I have something for you," he said as we stepped into his little hut.

"For me?"

"A bit early, but I'll miss the actual day once they start me at the outpost." He frowned a bit.

"My birthday?"

"Yes."

"I thought we agreed that nothing significant happens after about a century."

He scoffed as he guided me to the table. "I never agreed with what you said." I sat in the terrible little chair despite his protests that I should take the more comfortable one. Before sitting himself, he pulled a small basket from under the bed and placed the contents in front of me.

"Gaius," I gasped, finding a pillowy meringue pie in front of me. "Is it ..."

"Yes. Lemon and lavender."

Tears prickled. The depth of the gesture slammed into me like a boulder. "How did you know? About either the pie or my birthday?"

"I shouldn't give away my very reliable source, but the credit belongs to Imogen. She's been very helpful giving me ideas where you're concerned, Little Dove."

He turned to pull silverware out of the basket as well, and I realized what he meant. "She told you about the chocolates and the tea."

A grin spread across his face. "She did. I would love to claim that I guessed that well, but I did not. For days I wondered what she was talking about since she threw random things out in conversation. But then when I realized, I appreciated the insight. Very much."

I accepted a fork and wasted no time cutting a slice, opting to just scoop out a bite instead. "It was a good apology, Gaius." The fluffy meringue top melted on my tongue, sweet to the sharp lemon and earthy lavender. "And this is perfect," I sighed.

He copied me, filling his fork and rolling the bite around thoughtfully in his mouth, his brow furrowed as though he was trying to decide whether or not he liked the flavor.

"It's unusual. But not bad."

"Like us?" I teased. My bond pulsed in my chest, and I couldn't help but smile at this frustratingly handsome, stubborn man the fates had given me.

He snorted, revealing a charming lopsided grin I was growing incredibly fond of seeing and said, "Yes. Just like us, Little Dove."

Want a little more time with Gaius and Lovette?
Get the bonus scene by visiting:

https://BookHip.com/QSDKRBH

What's next?
Grab Book 3 of The Demon Princes Series,
The Demon's Delight for Seir's story!

Want to be the first to hear breaking news and
other info from L.? Sign up for her newsletter!

http://bit.ly/ALANewsletter

You can also join her reader group to chat
with her and other readers!

https://bit.ly/LilysReaderLounge

Did you like *The Gargoyle's Gift*? Leave a review
on Amazon, Goodreads or Bookbub to share
your thoughts with other readers!

ACKNOWLEDGEMENTS

As a writer who has tried a million times to become a plotter but always ends up writing by the seat of my pants, this story surprised me in all the best ways. Having the Oh. Is that what's happening? Moments is my favorite! I hope you loved Gaius and Lovette even half as much as I do!

Huge thanks as always to my husband for always being my first reader, just staring back when I glare in response to 'when do I get to read it' and making sure I don't drive myself crazy over unimportant details. I love you.

My Write or Die friends, Shain & Dannie, I heart you guys. I would not be where I am without you!

Krista, Jessica & Stephanie you always make my stuff so PRET-TY! I couldn't do it without your help and I mean that.

Beta & ARC readers! Do you even know how vital you are to authors like me? I hope you do. You're the bees knees and I cannot express how grateful I am to you! Seeing any post with my stuff on it is a humbling, thrilling experience. I couldn't do this without you. <3

I can't wait for you all to see what's coming next! There are more demons to make fall in love, and some stone kin I can't wait to help find their mates.

Note: This world is planned to be seven books, one for each brother PLUS a novella for our stone kin friends in-between. I hope you stick with us!

For sneak peeks, discussion and other fun tidbits, make sure you're signed up for my newsletter, & join my reader group.

ABOUT THE AUTHOR

L. Alexander writes Paranormal and Fantasy romance with sweet & spicy cinnamon roll heroes, fated mates, monsters, magic and more. She guarantees a happily ever after no matter what and has a soft spot for broody anime characters.

www.authorlilyalexander.com

@lilyalexanderwrites on Instagram

Lily Alexander on Facebook, TikTok, BookBub and Goodreads

L. also writes Contemporary Romance under the name Lily Alexander.

www.ingramcontent.com/pod-product-compliance
Lightning Source LLC
Chambersburg PA
CBHW031055310726
48969CB00007B/2289